CLAIMED BY THE MAFIA KING

THE MAFIA KINGS

BOOK THREE

BELLA MOONDRAGON

For Don

CONTENTS

1

———

TOMORROW AND EVERY DAY
AFTER

Eleni

I ROLL over in the thin cot, my whole body aching, and stare blearily at the dull gray ceiling.

The crack in one corner looks like it might've grown another millimeter since I last checked. Not that I know how long it's been.

There are no windows in here and just one heavy, metal door without even one of those little, barred windows you always see in movies to give me a clue what time it is. Camila dropped me off days or hours or months ago, and I haven't seen her since. I push myself up to sit, intending to do whatever kind of exercise I can in here to pass the time or keep in shape for whatever empty opportunity I get.

So far, all opportunities have been met with beatings. Bruises collect on my body between bright incisions where the edge of a nightstick or gun caught me.

My stomach twists. I lurch to my feet, stumble a few steps, and fall to my knees in front of the flat approximation of a toilet they allow me in here, the only furniture other than my cot. My breakfast—or lunch, or dinner—splatters noisily against the plastic. I've grown used

1

to the burn of bile. They feed me the same food for every meal, and whatever it is, it doesn't seem to agree with me. I wipe my mouth on the increasingly stained sleeve of my shirt and slump against the floor.

In my mind's eye, I picture the diner upstate Dante took me to that one day. The food I ordered was good, but I'm craving something Dante pointed out to me on the menu called disco fries. Thick, brown gravy drenches the potatoes, dripping off the half-melted mozzarella cheese curds. I wasn't brave enough to order them last time. Now, they make my mouth water with want.

Fuck, I might actually be losing it.

With effort—more every day, though I'm trying not to think about that—I imagine Dante's face. The hard planes of his cheeks and jaw. The darkness of his eyes that rivals the night sky. His matching hair, and the soft curls in it he tries to hide like they betray a secret softness to him. Tired worry and anger floods my veins. I don't know how long I've been here, I don't know how I'm getting out, but I know that I am. Between Dante and I, no one in the world could keep me forever.

The door creaks open, and I lean up on my elbow slowly in fear of pissing off my stomach again. It grumbles but doesn't formally revolt. A broad, clean-cut guard I haven't seen before steps in with the usual plastic lunch tray of food. He takes in my position on the floor, then the reeking mess in the "toilet."

"I can come back, if you're too sick now," he says.

I blink. That's…not how this usually goes. More often than not, a heavily tattooed, Russian-accented man tosses the tray on the floor, sending the bread sliding away and spilling some of the water on the pale chicken in the middle, regardless of how pathetic I've looked. They never offered to come back. This guy doesn't even really sound like he has an accent.

"Uh, no," I say, more to keep him in the room than anything else. Despite the fact my trays have no more cutlery than a thin paper cup, every single guard has watched me eat, like I could craft a weapon from rotisserie chicken and white bread.

I already would have, if I could.

He sets the tray down and backs up a few feet. I scuttle over to it. I don't even want to picture myself anymore. The well-dressed, recently groomed version of myself Gianna and I invented is long dead. I must look feral as I tear into the chicken with my hands and wash it down with sips of the glass of water they provide with every meal and no other time. The food might be what's making me sick, but with all my throwing up, I'm nearly constantly ravenous. I can't miss the opportunity to gain any strength I can.

"How are you?" the guard asks.

I laugh, my mouth full. Mama would be horrified. The guard just nods.

"I guess that's fair enough."

A heavy curtain of silence falls between us. I glance up at him from time to time, both waiting for him to pull a weapon and yank away the slim veneer of comfort he offers, and try to figure out what the hell he is.

He wears the same clothes as the Russians, mostly. But his wife beater bears fewer stains, and his track pants don't scrape against each other with the same plastic shriek.

His sneakers...God, I could really be losing my mind, but they look like they're made of two different shoes. From my angle below him on the floor, I can see thick, unworn soles that contrast the wear of the tops and laces.

A gun juts casually out of his waistband, and a heavy club I've seen cops use dangles out of his pocket, but he doesn't reach for either of them. I have no clue what's happening, but I can't really make things worse. The bruises from my last few attempts to learn anything keep gathering friends no matter what I do.

"What day is it?" My voice is a rasp that almost scares me.

He wets his lips. "I can't tell you."

"What's your name?" I try instead.

"Yagdash." He smiles. The word sounds strange in his mouth, like the corners and angles of it don't quite fit.

"I don't believe you," I mutter before cramming the last of my slice of bread into my mouth.

Either he didn't hear me, or he doesn't want to respond. Both are fine with me. My frantic mind spins out on the possibility he's some capo I haven't met, an agent of Dante's sent to save me. I can't blow his cover. Or—I glance up at "Yagdash"—someone from the Irish Kings, or the triads. Another organization trying to swoop in while I'm vulnerable. The way he clips his words could be hiding another accent, but he looks too white for the triads to allow him membership.

If I keep my mind sharp, even as my body dissolves around me, I might survive this. And I have to survive long enough for the escape I know is coming.

"You didn't finish your chicken," Yagdash says evenly.

I glance at the completely empty tray. Not even a drop of water remains. With a scowl, I grab the plastic and flip it upside down to prove him wrong.

My heart leaps. There, scratched on the back of weak plastic, sit two words. *Hang on.*

"Ah, can't be doing that." Yagdash grabs the tray, the cup that fell off it, and the full "toilet," then leaves the room without another word.

When the metal door slams shut behind him, I lean against the side of my cot and dig my nails into my palms. Hang on. Just a little longer.

2

KNIFE'S EDGE

DANTE

I SLAM my fist down on the counter, making the cat statue with its paw in the air topple over. "That's not fucking good enough."

Wing, the boss of the biggest triad in Chinatown, looks at me without a flicker of emotion in his eyes. "You storm into my shop. You set your goon outside to scare away reputable customers. And then you tell me I haven't met your expectations?"

I suck in a breath and grab for the fraying remains of my hold on my temper. A week and a half. She's been gone for a week and a half, and I'm not any goddamn closer than I was the night she disappeared.

If I didn't know about the three armed bruisers behind the curtain in this stupid fucking tea shop Wing and I both know handles a paltry portion of their money laundering, I'd already have my gun out. As is, I glance at Tony through the plate-glass store windows and remind myself he can't get in here fast enough.

"Is there anything else?" I ask, not bothering to keep the strain of desperation out of my voice.

"No." Wing stares down his nose at me. "A dozen Russian

monsters stormed my warehouse. They destroyed at least as many of my people, and more product. None can identify them because none lived. Trust me, Dante, I would have these Russians already in hand if I could."

"And Eleni?" Saying her name feels like scraping a razor blade along my vocal cords. A week and a half. I don't even know what they could be doing to her right now.

He cocks his head to the side and studies me for a long moment. "Your warehouse 42C shares a wall with one of mine, one I've been looking to expand. If I were to gain access to—"

"Done." I shove my hand out in front of me to shake on it. "It's yours if you tell me anything you find out and turn her over to me if you find her first."

Wing's first smile of the meeting curves his lips. He shakes my hand. "Now that we're partners, I'll admit one more thing. Those Russians peeled out of the docks headed north."

I thank him profusely, bob a quick bow as my father taught me when dealing with the triads, and storm out of the tea shop.

Tony falls into step beside me as soon as I exit. Exhaustion blurs his normally sharp features. I've sent nearly all of the Saints to ground as the Russians tear a hole through this goddamn city, but I couldn't give him up. I know it's selfish. Seb hasn't even been buried yet. But without my caporegime, I would come completely unglued.

"Anything?" he asks.

"They headed north," I hiss. "The Russians should be holed up in Brighton, where they'll blend."

"You can't exactly put those tattooed motherfuckers on the Upper East Side." Tony clenches and unclenches his fists. Like me, he's barely slept. We are more fury and caffeine than men, but maybe that's what we need.

I nod. "I'm thinking upstate."

Tony snarls. "That bitch would make it hard on us."

That bitch being Camila. The Russians are playing hardball with the city's drug trade, but they're barely bothering to do more than take out the people they find in other syndicate hideouts. The only reason El would be missing is if Camila took her. Chasing the Russians might take me from their boss to her, but if I can just get close enough, she can't fucking hide from me. Not now.

My phone rings. I slide it out of my pocket and surreptitiously check the caller ID. Tony and I have been living in each other's back pockets, sleeping in my office more often than not, but I haven't told him about my deal with Henry. I'll milk the fucking fed for all he's worth, but I don't need to drag Tony through the mud with me. The only clock on his hunt is his revenge. I need to find El.

Unknown number. Outer boroughs area code. I pick up.

"Dante," Cal's normally loose brogue sounds tight. "I come bearing gifts."

We reach the car. I slide into the driver's seat and put my phone on speaker instantly.

"What kind of gifts?" I ask.

"The Eastern European sort you're so hungry for," Cal replies.

Tony's scowl deepens. My heart skips a beat.

"Found a bar," Cal continues. "Old Russian hangout. Upscale thing, penthouse."

"How the fuck are you getting into a penthouse bar?" I throw the car into drive and peel away. If Cal doesn't have a plan worth explaining, I still need to get back to Staten Island fast enough to gear up for a proper raid and return.

"Owner's a friend of a friend." I can hear the bitter smile in his voice. "It turns out they're not much fonder of their tenants than we are."

"Count us in," I say. "When?"

"Tonight."

I hiss a breath through my teeth and press the pedal closer to the floor, bobbing and weaving through traffic.

"Sorry, gentlemen, you haven't given me reason to trust you in planning stages," Cal says. "If you were willing to talk about a partnership—"

"We'll be there," I spit.

"Grand." Cal hangs up before I can.

I start to coax the car faster and faster, the engine whining, but then the dashboard clock blares the time. I'm going to be late if I go home now. I slam the brakes and spin into a turn, sending Tony knocking against the door. Two more sharp corners, and I park in front of Lou's Deli.

Tony looks at the secret headquarters we've always held on this side of the bridge, then at me. "You know some bar raid isn't going to tell you shit."

My temper strains at my weakening hold. "You don't know shit."

"It's Cal Duncan," Tony says tiredly. "He'd shoot at clouds if the rain pissed him off."

"Cal is a lunatic." I squeeze the wheel. "He runs the Kings with an iron fist, and I wouldn't spend an evening with him if I had another goddamn way. Right now, he's got a lick of territory and a quarter of the manpower the Russians have, but he has an *in*, which we don't. "

Tony looks at Lou's again. "What did you promise Wing?"

Like a pricked balloon, all my righteous rage dribbles out of me. A week and a half of stealing half-hours of sleep on the couch I first fucked Eleni on slam into me like a fist to the gut. I'm so goddamn tired. I just want to find Eleni and take her home. No, not even that. I want to take her far, far away from here, where no one has ever heard our names.

"I have a meeting," I say. "I'll pick you up in a couple hours. Be ready."

Tony doesn't say anything as he gets out of the car, but the way he slams the door tells me everything I need to know. Seb is sitting on ice in a funeral home somewhere, waiting for Tony to have five fucking minutes to bury him, and I'm dropping Tony off to be babysat.

I pull away from the curb. I can't be late.

3

———

CRACKS

Eleni

Another millimeter on that crack in the ceiling. Or maybe the same millimeter as last time. If the cot were a little higher, I could trace it with my fingers. Yagdash hasn't been back in three meals, and I don't know whether I dreamed his message anymore.

"—the fuck do you mean, no?" a woman shrieks.

I lever myself up on an elbow. I haven't heard a woman's voice since Camila last left.

"I need more protection here!" The voice grows louder, as if approaching, and I realize it is Camila. "Are you fucking listening to me? At least half a dozen men."

Someone murmurs a response, but their voice is too low for me to hear. Their statement ends in a *thud* I can't make sense of from inside my concrete cell.

"Last night, those fucking redheaded gnats hit the White Winter. We lost people. And I put my ass on the line, promising the White Winter was fucking untouchable," she yells. "That means they're closing in."

"No," the other voice rumbles. "It means *your* ass is on the line. He's not going to be happy with this request."

Camila shrieks, a wordless, animal rage. I cling to the details. White Winter doesn't mean anything to me, but the red-headed gnats have to be the Irish Kings. They probably found a Russian site. I lean forward, hoping to hear anything about Dante and the Saints.

"Tell him whatever the fuck you want," she shouts. "I know what I fucking need to run this operation, and he knows I know. Just get it done!"

The door to my cell slams open, and I drop back against the bed as fast as I can.

"Don't waste my fucking time," Camila spits.

She slams the door shut behind her, and I twist my head to look at her without getting up. She's wearing wide, barely blue pants and a matching blouse, but the blouse hangs slightly out of her waistband and her hair is loose. She looks wild, her eyes burning. I shouldn't test her right now. So I sit up slowly, willing my stomach to remain calm.

"Why are you—"

Mistake. Camila whips one of those heavy batons out of a pale holster I didn't notice, hers nearly clear compared to the black sticks of the other guards, and charges me with a scream. I throw my hands up, and her first blow lands on my forearms. The bones jar, but she doesn't hit nearly as hard as the massive Russian men I've been holding up against.

"You're not worth it!" She reels back and swings at my side.

Praying my stomach holds up, I roll under her blow and off the cot. Nausea claws at my throat, but I resist it to barrel into her legs. She topples to the floor with a string of curses. I should climb on top of her and take control, but I have to breathe in and out through my nose a few times or vomit.

Camila takes advantage of my hesitation and slams her baton into my shoulders. "You don't even know what you have! You're wasting it!"

The perfect picture of Dante I keep inscribing in my mind, planning for however long she keeps me, burns in my mind's eye. A smile softens his severe face, and I remember his admission that he had a whole plan for his proposal but couldn't resist asking me.

Who gives a fuck if I throw up on Camila Donato?

As she looms over me for another blow, I channel all my training, with and without Dante. I slam my foot into her stomach, making her crumple, and then crunch her nose under my fist. She goes down with a shriek, and I roll on top of her.

My stomach riots. I ignore it to bruise her perfect cheekbone, to try to knock one of her glistening teeth out. She loses her hold on the baton and claws at my arms. The bright lines of pain only spur my indolent anger to a fiery rage. I knock her head to the side one more time, then realize I'm wasting my time. Her slim, golden throat is right there.

I lock my hands around her windpipe. Her eyes go wide.

"I used to be just like you!" she wheezes.

I roll my eyes and try to find the part of her throat that crushes her vocal cords.

"I got pulled into this life." She sinks her stiletto-sharp nails into the backs of my hands. "I know what it's like to go from innocent to unable to get out without dying."

"I don't want to get out." I squeeze harder. Her eyes bulge.

"You don't have to!" Her voice is a thin whisper of air. "I can show you how to—to be more. To reach the top of whoever has the power."

"I thought you wanted Dante."

She squirms underneath me like a worm. Hot, vibrant power courses through me. Her fragile life is in my hands.

"I want to survive," she wheezes, "just like you do. Work with me. I can protect you, and we can share his body in the aftermath."

I adjust my hands one last time, and that seems to be the right position. Camila falls silent, fighting weakly. Her nails barely break my skin. Her punches don't even bruise. She falls limp in my grasp. A few seconds more, and she'll be dead. I'll have killed her with my bare hands, nothing like shooting Luca or calling for all those deaths in the aftermath.

My stomach wrenches. I lurch off Camila and vomit. When it's done, I feel hollow, shaky. She remains motionless behind me. Bright-red handprints, my handprints, mar her skin. Even like this, it would be easy to climb on top of her and finish the job.

I slump to the concrete floor and stare up at the ceiling. The one crack in the corner seems to have shrunk from this angle. Long minutes dribble away.

Camila coughs. I twist my head to look at her.

"If I were you," she says, "I'd care a lot more about my survival now."

I raise an eyebrow.

She gets to her feet. Dirt mars her perfect outfit, but she straightens it anyway. "Your life is tied to the baby's. So I guess that's the question—the two of you, or Dante?"

4

SLEEPING WITH THE DEVIL

DANTE

I SLIDE into the booth in the tiny, barely-Brooklyn diner across from Henry Alcott and a man I don't know, and I think about killing them here and now.

We agreed to be subtle about this. I picked a place outside of any territory worth talking about. I changed in the car, into one of the patterned button-downs I only keep for the barbecue and a pair of shorts. And here these two assholes sit with their high-and-tights, cop shoes squeaking on the stained linoleum, badges and guns bulging their crap impersonation of what normal people wear to lunch. They need to know who the fuck they're dealing with, and that I'm not fucking around anymore.

"Who the fuck are you?" I ask the stranger with no preamble.

He prickles. "All right, dickhead, you—"

Henry holds his hand out between us. "This is Jace Covett. He's...a friend."

"Covett." I roll the name around in my mouth. The shape of it is familiar to me. "There was a Covett in the remains of Thano Coppola's books."

"Don't fucking say that name," he hisses.

I snort and lean back, pleased with the confirmation of his guilt. Fucking dirty cops. "Easy enough. By the way, Henry, I heard you just got transferred here from Chicago."

"I did," he says slowly. "Why?"

"No reason." I shake my head with a smile. "Just funny, cause I also heard the key witness in the Luciano case died before he could take the stand."

Henry pales a few shades. "Did he?"

I nod slowly. "The whole case is falling apart. And they really thought they had Luciano this time too."

The waitress wanders over, takes our orders between snapping her gum and texting, and wanders away.

"Now that we're all on the same page"—I cross my arms, just barely revealing the strap of a shoulder holster in the neck of my shirt —"what do you have?"

"Something solid." Henry taps on the edge of the table. "Couple months back, Jace placed an asset in a pack of Russian dealers upstate."

My heart hammers. The waitress drags over three cups of black coffee, all lukewarm. I suck mine down without tasting it.

"The asset is…let's say a go-getter," Henry continues. "Soared up the chain. Not close enough to the boss for a name, but close enough to touch the New York syndicate already."

"And I'd rather not risk his cover on this bullshit," Jace mutters.

"We won't," Henry says with the finality of an argument they've already had a dozen times.

I can barely focus on all this goddamn backstory. I don't care about assets or dealers upstate. I want to know where El is, and I want to know now. I'm vibrating in a way that has nothing to do with the coffee.

"Cut to the fucking chase, or the director will find a very interesting letter on his desk come morning," I say.

Jace starts forward like he's going to hit me, but Henry stops him. I offer my most shit-eating grin.

"Long story short, he found her," Henry says. "Eleni. And she's alive."

All the breath whooshes out of my body in a single gust. My ears feel like they're ringing. *Alive.* I'll get to touch her again, taste her lips, apologize for leaving her.

I nod like I'm not coming apart at the seams. "So when are we going?"

"We?" Jace sneers. "I wouldn't go anywhere with you."

I don't give a fuck about his attitude anymore. It rolls off my shoulders under the soporific whirlpool of the knowledge Eleni's alive.

"The asset can get her out of danger during the FBI's raid," Henry says.

"I can get her the fuck out of danger," I reply. "Give me the goddamn address. I'll end it tonight. She's upstate, right?"

Jace and Henry exchange looks. I think about knocking their heads together. Our food arrives, and absolutely none of it is what we ordered.

"If you're involved in the raid, you will be arrested," Henry says with all the finality of a cell door slamming shut. "Our credentials protect Jace and I. You're just another wanted criminal."

"You fucking pigs," I snarl. "Tell me where she is, or I'll—"

Jace grabs for his gun, Henry for his badge.

"Or you'll what?" Henry says. "I could write just as lovely a letter as you. That house of yours is looking nice, by the way."

Goddammit. My temper strains to bursting at the edges of my control. I need—

"Fine," I spit. "Then I don't give a fuck about getting arrested. Lock me up and throw away the key. I need to fucking see her."

Henry and Jace exchange another glance. I claw onto the edge of the table instead of shooting them both.

"You can't fucking tell him," Jace says in a near whisper. "This is what he's like now. It's like unhooking a rabid dog's chain."

"I'm right fucking here," I reply.

Henry shakes his head. "No, it's not. I grew up with him. I grew up in this life. I know what the news is going to mean."

"What the fuck are you talking about?" I seethe, looking from man to man.

"Watch your fucking language, you Italian prick–"

"You don't need your dick to raid some warehouse," I press. "I have a fucking knife, and I'm happy to show you how good I am."

"Enough," Henry says sternly.

Jace's jaw works. "I think you're an idiot." He eyes Henry before lowering his gaze to his fists.

"And yet, I've got six months of seniority on you." Henry turns back to me with a perfectly placid smile that makes me want to knock his teeth in. "Where they're keeping her, someone has seen fit to knock Eleni out a few times and submit her to doctor's visits."

"What?"

"They're monitoring her condition," Henry says patiently, "because she's a little over a month pregnant."

The diner falls away. My blood roars in my ears. Pregnant. My Eleni, lost somewhere in the world, carrying our first child. She's going to be beautiful with pregnancy. My spinning mind constructs a vision of her; glowing, belly bulging, swatting me and telling me it's my job as the husband to get her whatever she wants. A taut, fragile smile pulls on my cheeks. Son or daughter, I'll love them. Oh, I'll spoil them senseless.

Reality crashes back down on me with aching certainty. I can't spoil anyone from jail. I can't risk my life or my freedom on this raid. I need to make sure I'm here for Eleni and our child. I exhale, long and slow, then open eyes I don't remember closing. Henry is watching me closely, his eyebrows pinched. Jace is shaking his head.

"Okay," I say. "I'll stay out of the raid itself, somewhere nearby, and I won't pull heroics at the last second. What's the plan?"

Henry grins.

5

IT CAN'T BE

ELENI

I PACE the few steps back and forth in my tiny concrete cell, trying to keep my thoughts in order. Somewhere outside, someone made something with cabbage, and the reek of it is making it hard to think. But I need to focus. If I can count all the meals I've had, maybe I can figure out how long I've been here, and then I'll know whether Camila was lying about the baby.

Nine meals since Yagdash and the message. I think. Or was it ten? No, eight. Okay, that's too far. I've had one meal since I woke up. Before that....

I sit down with a groan. Counting is impossible down here, and the stench is only making it worse! My period has always been regular. Dante and I used protection. Surely, I'll know when I'm pregnant.

Deep in the darkest recesses of my mind, I kind of hope I'm not. I can picture a family with Dante someday, but if I'm pregnant now, and Camila knows, she's going to find a way to make me choose between the baby and him. I just know it.

Muffled by the thick cement walls around me, a car backfires. I whip my head up. I haven't heard anything that wasn't nearby. Maybe within the hallway I'm on. And there's no way there's a car back here, so that's…gunfire.

Again. My heart races. Dante found me. I smooth my hair, scrub my sleeve over my mouth. It's impossible to even keep track of the last time I threw up. Then, I climb to my feet and ready myself.

The door screeches open. I start to smile. Camila sprints in, her white sundress spattered with bright-red blood and a wild look in her eye.

"Too late." She cackles and swings the gun in her hand toward me.

Toward my stomach.

Some new instinct, hot and bright, overwhelms me, and I dive away just as she pulls the trigger. It's not graceful. I land in a heap, curled around my center protectively. The door stands open a few feet away, but between the metallic stink of blood and that goddamn cabbage, I can barely move without puking. Camila turns slowly, still laughing.

"I gave you the option." She takes careful aim. "But you don't know how to—"

Bullets fly in through the open door. Camila leaps for cover, turning my cot on its side. I crane my neck as much as I can just in time to see Yagdash step inside, now wearing a bulletproof vest.

"Come on," he says. "We have to move."

Helpless tears fill my eyes. "I-I can't—"

He glances at me for a second. "Fuck. Okay." Yagdash stuffs his weapon into his belt and scoops me off the ground in one smooth move.

I clap a hand to my mouth. When Camila captured me, I was able to fight. I was dangerous. I was someone Cal Duncan wanted to meet. And now, I'm just some girl trying not to puke on the man she thinks is rescuing her.

Yagdash charges out of the cement room and into the surrounding basement. The dirt floor kicks up puffs of dust under his feet, and a handful of Russians lay bleeding already. I look behind us and see the concrete cell I've been living in is one of a few in a line but clearly a new addition to this ancient basement.

He hits the stairs. I twist and puke over his arms. He curses again but doesn't stop, something I think I'll always be grateful for. The cabbage smell grows more and more overpowering.

We exit the stairs into an old-looking kitchen. Faded wooden cabinets. A pot of something noxious on the stove. A metal table, stained and burned with years of use. My stomach seizes like it wants to puke again but doesn't have anything left. Yagdash doesn't hesitate, just runs toward where I can still hear gunshots. I cling to his arm and wrap my other hand around my stomach, like that'll protect anything that might be in there.

"Covering fire!" Yagdash hollers into what I just noticed is a headset. My fingers drift over the bright white letters on his vest. "I'm coming out."

The gunfire increases, but with more of the telltale sound of bullets hitting wood and drywall. A soft, white dust filters down from the ceiling as Yagdash sprints past a wallpapered staircase and out the open front door. I suck in my first breath of clean air—

And choke on it. The overgrown lawn disappears under the sheer number of people in full tactical gear, all emblazoned with a bright, white "FBI." My chest constricts, squeezing all the air out of my lungs. My hand on his arms starts shaking. Dante's been arrested. I'm being arrested. It's all over. I'm never even going to get to say goodbye to Mama.

"Don't tell them anything," Yagdash mutters.

He drops me on a stretcher, and a small army of EMTs swarm me before I can ask anything. Only the clouds overhead whisking past and the deafening rattling tell me the stretcher is moving. I can't feel anything anymore. It's over.

"—lo." One of the EMTs tries to meet my gaze. "Hello, miss, I need to ask you a few questions."

My breath rasps out of my throat. Oh, god.

"How many fingers am I holding up?" He offers me three fingers.

"Th-th-three." My teeth chatter, nearly catching my tongue. Was I in that room until winter came? Why am I so cold?

Shock. This is shock. I feel it creeping into my bones.

"Are you injured anywhere?" he asks.

The baby. I don't know. I open and close my mouth, trying to shape uncertain words. He nods worriedly and begins attaching clamps and wires to me. Something starts beeping. I raise up, and then the sky disappears, replaced by the textured metal ceiling of an ambulance.

We're moving now. The vibration beneath from the tires tearing over bumpy, unkempt payment has my head lolling as fresh nausea sweeps through me, blurring my senses.

The EMTs talk amongst themselves, attach more things to me. A sharp needle enters my arm, but I only notice it by its shine in the air above me. They have Dante. They have me. They have the baby. There is nothing left of my family.

The ambulance skids to a stop. That seems soon. A yard like that wouldn't happen anywhere populous. Then, the back doors open, and I scream.

Dante steps in. Exhausted, the lines on his face more prominent than ever, wrinkled like a used tissue, but Dante is here. I fight the grasps and restraints of the EMTs, weeping openly.

He brandishes a gun. "All right, we're gonna do this nice and simple. My friend up front has direction. If you take us there, leave enough equipment to take care of her, and go, we won't have any problems."

The EMT who asked me about his fingers frowns. "She's not seriously injured, but—"

"I will take care of her!" Dante bellows. "Drive or die. Those are your choices."

The EMT nods. Distantly, I hear Tony giving directions, and the ambulance starts moving. My breath feels less like it's fighting me. Dante sits next to me.

"Oh, El," he says like I'm a damaged heirloom.

Still, he kisses me like I'm the most beautiful thing he's ever seen.

6

───────

REPERCUSSIONS

Dante

I sit in an armchair I dragged into the master bedroom in my safe house upstate, watching Dr. Fletcher and his nurse tend to El. She looks so small in the bed, the hollows of her cheeks sunken and her hair lank. Not seriously injured, the EMT said. Still, I'm thrilled I had enough time to hire Fletcher and the nurse before the raid. They're discreet, professional, and fast. They talk to each other in snippets of conversation that give me the barest hint of what's going on.

"Saline. Her veins are shrunken."

"Heart rate elevated, but not dangerously."

"That laceration is likely infected. We need penicillin and a disinfectant."

I don't dare interrupt them. I can't imagine stealing a second Eleni might need to get better. Tear streaks mark her face, and she was already crying when I got in the ambulance. In the end, Camila had her in that fucking house for two weeks. Two goddamn weeks. I am counting my blessings she's not in more danger, but I'm fucking terrified.

21

Tony leans in the doorway. "Dante, I need to talk to you."

"Fuck off," I say without any heat, without looking away from El.

"Now." Tony's voice holds a note of iron I almost never hear from him.

I twist. My best friend, my caporegime, is pale with an expression I've never seen before.

El makes a small, pained noise, and I whip back around. "Talk here or wait."

Tony grabs my arm and hauls me out of the chair. "Fucking now."

I'm too stunned to do anything but stumble after him. Sure, we've fought, even physically. We grew up side-by-side. But he's never touched me like this before. Tony rips open the door to a random guest bedroom and shoves me inside.

"Henry Alcott led that raid," Tony says.

My stomach drops. He's putting it together.

"So?" I ask.

He scoffs. "You think I'm fucking stupid. Great. I put my kid brother's fucking funeral on hold to follow your sorry ass around the city, and you want to treat me like a goddamn secretary."

"I don't think you're stupid." My temper is exhausted from control, drained and hapless, but it starts to stir anyway. "I made you my fucking caporegime, didn't I? And you know good and well Seb deserves a capo's funeral, with everyone around him."

Crack. Tony backhands me. The hit only barely registers as pain. Bone-deep shock radiates out from the point where I feel my cheek split and a thin ribbon of blood drizzle down.

"You don't say his name until I bury him," Tony says. "It's not yours."

I bite back the retort that I watched him grow up just the same as Tony did. There is something in the ice-blue eyes of my best friend that I don't recognize. I don't wipe the blood away either.

"Once," I say. "You can do that *once* because I know what you're going through. Touch me like that again, and you'll regret it."

We stare at each other for a long moment, violence crackling between us like lightning strikes. Tony has his gun. I don't.

"When they took Eleni," I start.

Tony scoffs. "It's always fucking her, isn't it? Shit, Dante, I'm starting to think Uncle John was right."

I draw myself up to my full height. "Fifteen years together. That's why I'm not taking your fucking gun from you right now. I am your don, Antony Bellini, and it would do you well to remember that."

Tony's jaw works. "Fine. Give me your fucking story."

"None of my men had anything." I begin circling Tony with the same crisp bearing. He at least has the training not to watch me. "I'd just left you on the street, covered in blood. And fucking Henry Alcott turned up, saying he was here to hunt the Russians' boss."

"Well, that's fucking handy," Tony mumbled.

I let that slide. For the last time.

"I said what he wanted to hear," I continue. "And then, I looked into our dear old friend Henry. He's here because of speed transfer. Before he left, he created a hole in an important witness' protection detail, just enough to scuttle the Luciano case in Chicago. He's dirty, and I can prove it with three phone calls. So I didn't promise him shit."

Tony huffs a breath. "But you're still in bed with him."

"Him and a colleague, Jace Covett, who belonged to Thano Coppola before his untimely end." I meet my old friend's gaze. "Because I deemed it best for the Staten Island Saints. And because I know how this goddamn looks, because I'm not as fucking stupid as you seem to think I am, I was *keeping you out of it*. I didn't want you in the mud with me."

"They're feds, sir," Tony says, though the *sir* seems to pain him. "You can't trust feds."

"And I don't." I stop in front of him. "I trust you. I trust our organization. And I will use any leg up I need to get us where we belong. *Capiche?*"

He nods sullenly.

"Go back to the city." I turn away from him. "Muster the capos. Make sure everyone is all right and tell them the time for hiding is over."

"You're dismissing me?" he asks, incredulous.

I whip back. "I'm giving you an order."

He holds my gaze for a long moment, then leaves the room. A second later, I hear the door to the house slam, followed by an engine turning over. I exhale, all the tension melting out of me. Tony and I have never disagreed like that before.

Dr. Fletcher's nurse knocks on the door frame. "Excuse me, Mr. Cattaneo?"

I shake myself and force a tired smile. "Yes?"

"Dr. Fletcher will see you now." She jerks her head back toward the master bedroom.

I smooth down my jacket. "Let's go."

She puts a hand up, then pulls a gauze out of one of the pockets of her smock and daubs my cheek. It comes away red, and I wince as her touch makes it pulsate.

"Shouldn't need a stitch, but I have bandages." She holds out a few paper packages.

"I'd rather not waste the time," I say honestly. "But thank you, Nurse...?"

"Adelaide." She smiles. "Come on."

We walk down the hallway in silence and return to the room where I left El. So much has changed in my absence. An IV stand sits next to the bed, drizzling something clear into her arm, and a beeping heart monitor stands on the other side. Thankfully, the monitor offers a steady *beep, beep, beep* that allows me to believe Eleni really is still alive, looking like this with her eyes closed. Dr. Fletcher brushes off his hands and steps over to join Adelaide and me.

"She's unconscious, on some pain meds. I don't suppose I need to tell you she's not in good condition." He smiles ruefully.

I shake my head, my heart hammering. "How bad is it?"

"Nothing she can't recover from, I believe." He looks over his shoulder and shakes his head. "She's a tough young woman, I'll tell you that."

"I know." I've never known anything more.

"She's dehydrated and extremely undernourished." He turns back to me. "But the thing to really keep an eye on is an incision on her ribs. Shallow, normally wouldn't be anything to look twice at, but she clearly wasn't bathing, so it's infected. We've got her on a basic course of antibiotics now"—he gestures to the IV—"but it's important to make sure that doesn't develop into something dangerous like sepsis."

I nod.

"Adelaide will be staying on to handle cleanings, changing bandages, and general care, but take it easy." Dr. Fletcher eyes me. "I mean that."

"I wouldn't risk her," I say fervently. "What about...the other thing I mentioned?"

He pulls a vial of blood from the pocket of his white coat. "I'll confirm the pregnancy as soon as I return to my office."

I exhale sharply. Part of me thought I'd get to know right away whether my baby had also been captured by the Russians for two weeks. But I can wait.

"I'm headed out," Dr. Fletcher says.

"And I'll give you some space." Adelaide smiles as the two of them leave the room together.

I drag the chair from the foot of the bed to the head, right next to the IV, and take El's hand. A single strip of her finger is paler than the rest, where her engagement ring used to sit. I don't think I've ever been angrier than the day the tracker led me to the Hudson. Without anything else to do, I pull my ring off and slide it onto her thumb, the only place it will fit.

"Never again, El," I whisper. "Or you, little one."

7

SUNSHINE

Eleni

I BLINK awake to something warm on my face. My stomach grumbles threateningly around its emptiness, and I start to sit up to find the bedpan.

Something restrains my left arm. Two somethings.

I turn slowly in the sun-drenched bed, fighting for enough memories to put together where I am. The first something is Dante, slumped in an armchair from the living room of the safe house upstate but still holding onto my hand. He looks actually, properly relaxed, his brow unlined for once. The sun sparkles off something in our entwined hands, and for a heart-racing moment, I think he found my engagement ring. But no, he's slipped his ring onto my thumb, where it barely fits. Tears fill my eyes as I manage a wobbly smile.

The second something is an IV full of clear liquid. Unlabeled bag. My arm aches—everything does—but I feel steadier than I have in ages. Like sleep actually refreshed me. I can even tell someone did something to my mouth because it tastes minty fresh instead of like old vomit. I suck in a breath of clean, free air. I'm safe.

27

I'm also starving, but that seems like a problem for later.

"Dante," I murmur. Anything louder than that would hurt my unused voice, I can tell.

His eyes shoot open, and panic mars his expression.

"I'm here," I say quickly. "I'm okay."

He scans my face, still worried, then cups my cheek as he relaxes. "El."

"Dante." The tears in my eyes spill.

He kisses me around them, gentle like he could break me at any second and hungry like he can only be certain I'm home when he's checked every inch of my body himself. I press up into him as much as I can, breathing in his scent and the safety that comes with it. Finally, muscles shaking, I slump back against the pillow.

"I love you," I say.

He kisses my knuckles. "I love you too. I missed you."

My laugh rasps out of my throat. "I missed a lot of things, but you were up there."

He grins down at me so wide it must hurt. I want to stay in this moment forever, in the first blush of reunion. But I have to ask.

"How long has it been?"

Dante's face shutters. "About two weeks. I'm so sorry."

I shake my head, tears still flowing. "You have nothing to be sorry for."

"Camila—"

I put my free hand to his lips, silencing him. "Nothing. You look like you haven't slept in two weeks. I bet you did everything you could."

He kisses my fingers. "I slept a little."

I sniffle and pull my hand back. "I think I can forgive that."

He laughs. "What else do you want to know?"

Two weeks. Nearly as long as I lost him for. Did he lose his mind without me? Is anyone thinking about the fact that the semester starts in less than a week, and moving seems impossible? The part of me that ran the Saints wants to ask how the syndicate is, how the city is. The part of me that's tired and sore wins out.

"Camila?" I ask.

Dante shakes his head. "In the wind."

I grimace. I could've grabbed Yagdash's gun and shot her. This could all be over.

"A handful of Russian capos were arrested, though," he says. "Enough that just taking out one or two of them won't be enough to clean up the mess."

I bite my lower lip. "There were feds everywhere. How did you take me without them finding you?" My heart skips a beat. "Or did they?"

Dante's gaze slides away from me for the first time since he's woken up. "They didn't, don't worry. You remember Henry Alcott?"

I nod. I'll never forget the slimy fed who nearly cornered Mama.

"He and his organized-crimes cronies are all over the city, taking down any syndicate that pops their head up for air," he says. "It was child's play to put a tail on one of them and wait until they led us somewhere useful."

I swallow. The action burns my acid-scarred throat, and my stomach reminds me it could end this lovely moment whenever it wants.

"Camila said—"

"I don't know if you—"

Dante and I both stop and laugh.

"You go." I don't want to bring up the potential of a baby until we've covered everything else.

He takes a deep breath. "I don't know if you know, but there was a doctor at the house who was checking you out...in case you were pregnant."

My breath catches. "I was going to ask if you knew. But I don't know if it's real." I curl my free arm around my stomach anyway.

"Nor me yet." He sighs. "But I had my own doctor draw your blood, and...well, did you get your period while you were in there?"

I shake my head. Wait, he said two weeks! I begin calculating in my head.

"You're late," Dante says before I finish. "By a significant amount of time."

Something warm washes through my chest. He's been paying attention. He's been counting.

Oh, my god, I might actually be pregnant. At twenty-four. Without a college degree to my name, hiding out in upstate New York. Oh, shit.

"What are we going to do?" I whisper.

"I'm going to make things safe for you." Sunshine highlights every dramatic angle of Dante's face, making him look more like a statue than a living, breathing man I can call mine. "You and our baby."

"We can't go home," I say. "The feds are everywhere, right? Have they found any Saints?"

Dante looks at me for a long moment. "No, they haven't."

I exhale. "Thank fuck. I haven't fixed everyone's computers yet."

"The feds aren't looking for the Saints." His gaze bores into me, trying to impress some meaning.

I shake my head in confusion.

"You were gone, El," Dante says slowly. "I needed to follow any lead I had back to you."

"O...kay?" I frown at him.

"I made a deal with Henry Alcott," he admits. "For now, we're safe."

My mouth falls open.

8

SECOND STRING

TONY

"CHECK ON THE FUCKING CAPOS," I mutter under the music as I soar down the Verrazano Bridge in the dead of night. "Call them back. Check in with Cal fucking Duncan. Take out my goddamn laundry while I play house upstate. I'm the don, don't forget."

In my mind, I hear Seb's response. *You sound like a cranky toddler, Tony. You two love each other. He's dealing with a lot. You'll be back to normal in no time.*

"He's dealing with a lot?" I demand. "I'm talking to my dead fucking brother in my mind as I drive to meet the head of the Irish Kings."

The Seb in my mind only shrugs. I win a lot more arguments since—

I crank the music to drown out my thoughts.

After weaving through city traffic, I pull up in front of McCreegan's Pub and leave the music blaring for a few extra seconds. May as well give the little dick something to complain about. Then, I shut off

31

the car and head inside. Just like last time, the bartender leads me through the freezer, into the second bar Cal installed in the back of his goddamn pub. Unlike last time, a few other Kings mill around, drinking, gambling, and playing darts. Cal still stands at the bar. I stride up to him.

"If I'd known we were partying, I would've eaten first."

Cal grins. "You're welcome to party with my lads, but I was rather thinking we might grab a drink and step aside."

I roll my eyes. "Whiskey."

With a teasing smile, he pours me a draught of that same black beer, then one for himself and leads me to a corner booth.

"You need new fucking ears," I mutter as I sit.

"I have heard that before." Cal draws a curtain around us that instantly deadens the sound of the rest of the secret bar. "Apologies for the crowd. We're staying close to home, which I'm sure you can understand."

I lift my glass to him and take a sip. I don't even hate dark beer like this, I just need something stronger to burn the words Dante said to me before I left from my head. In bed with the fucking FBI because his fiancée was missing for half an hour and we didn't have any leads yet. I could kill him.

"How were the *hinterlands*?" Cal asks pleasantly. "I heard about a kerfuffle."

I snort. "Federal raid. Russian house."

"Funny that you managed to be there." He glances up at me. "Isn't it?"

"How do you fucking figure?" I cross my arms. "You were the one who said Henry was leading the charge. That little dick is my cousin. I know him better than—" Seb's face pops into my mind, and I choke on my next inhale.

Catching my breath is a fucking fight. I haven't slept a night in weeks, and exhaustion is taking its revenge. The whole time, Cal looks on without lifting a pinkie to help. Fucking dick.

"I don't discount the power of blood," he says when I'm done. "Merely the power of coincidence." He sips his beer.

"Go to church if you want to talk doubt." I swig mine. "Half a dozen Russians in custody, and Dante has Eleni back, so I wouldn't expect him to pick up your calls much longer."

Cal nods slowly. "Ours was always a partnership of convenience. Where is the gentleman in question, anyway?"

"Taking care of Eleni," I say through gritted teeth.

He makes a small, understanding noise in the back of his throat. "I remember when my da started looking like he was ready to shuffle off. Tad nerve-wracking, looking at the driver's seat and knowing it's yours soon, hm?"

Every ounce of my willpower pours into not reacting to that statement. What the fuck does he mean, shuffling off? Dante's only had the Saints for five years, he's still going strong.

The memory of my fingers wrapped around his arm crashes through my thoughts. He *was* going strong. Now, when I tell him we have business to talk about, I hear "hold on" more often than "what's up?"

"Well, worry not." Cal raises his glass. "The Kings are happy to talk something more than a partnership of convenience, whenever your time does come. I like you better than Dante, anyway. We both have a little more of that old-fashioned street under our nails."

I stare at Cal's drink for a long moment and think about how long I've fought to hide the fact that Dante is this college-educated golden child, and I'm some Italian kid he pulled along for a ride. Then, I finish my beer and stand.

"Seems like that's a conversation to have when the time comes."

Cal laughs.

When I get in the car, I turn toward Staten Island. Let Dante figure out his shit upstate, if that's what he wants.

The Seb I keep imagining, stained with blood, appears in the passenger's seat next to me.

"Don't say it," I spit.

He needs you, he says anyway. *If it were you up there, he'd go.*

"The old Dante would've." I pull up to a T intersection. One way takes me to the highway. The other, the Verrazano Bridge to Staten Island. "These days, I don't fucking know."

Dude. Imaginary Seb turns to look at me, blood sputtering from his wounds.

With a sigh, I turn toward the highway.

LIKE A COMPLETE FUCKING FREAK, I knock on the front door of the safe house an hour later. I have keys. I've always just walked in. But it feels like a place I can't share anymore.

Dante opens the door. He's finally traded out his shitty, two-day-old suit for a T-shirt and sweatpants, but that makes him look even more unstrung. The small cut I put on his cheek stands out from the puffy flesh around it. For the first time since I've known him, he looks old.

"Tony," he says, suddenly guarded. "I wasn't expecting you back."

I push past him with an armful of groceries. "Oh yeah? What was your food plan?"

Dante opens and closes his mouth a few times. "I hadn't gotten there yet."

Used to be, he didn't miss a beat. I head for the kitchen and start unpacking.

"I changed my mind," he says. "We should keep low."

"I know." I load vegetables into the empty fridge. "I already told the guys that. Gave 'em money to stay under."

"Good." Dante nods. "I'm sor—"

I put up a hand. "Are you done with the feds?"

After a long pause, he says, "I don't think I can be yet."

I force my hand down to my side despite the sick emotions begging me to hit him again. "Don't apologize to me until that's true."

He swallows loud enough that I can hear it. "Fine."

"How's Eleni?" I ask because I know Seb would.

"She's going to be fine." Dante walks up next to me and begins helping. "But I can't keep her hidden here forever, Tone."

I catch Dante's eye, and I know. There's no way this ends without Dante burning down the Russians for what they did to Eleni.

Or worse, disappearing with her forever.

9

COUNTRY AIR

Eleni

"Let me get that." Dante swoops into my path and tries to grab the full plate of pasta out of my hands.

I hold on with a small smile. "I've been walking for two days. I think I can handle carrying my own dinner."

"You are stubborn." He kisses the tip of my nose. "Can I take your glass instead?"

I nod, and he lets go. He's been doting on me for the last three days, barely letting me do anything.

It's sweet, but it's also driving me insane. I pad from the kitchen into the living room and sit on the couch. Dante's pasta and his glass of wine wait on the coffee table. I set mine next to his, and a moment later, he appears with my glass of sparkling apple juice. We both look at it for a moment. Dr. Fletcher hasn't called yet. I haven't gotten my period yet. Without talking about it, Dante and I both agreed I'm not going to drink until we know one way or the other.

"What do you want to watch tonight?" I ask, shattering the spell.

He passes me the glass and blinks a few times. "I picked last night. It's your turn."

I grab the remote, my muscles still ache but it's definitely better. And I've gotten good at containing the wince that makes Dante worry. I really am fine.

"No complaints?" I ask.

He sighs, trying to look put-upon, but the smile tugging at his lips betrays him. I put on a rom-com I've seen a thousand times and settle in. Despite my injuries and the other lingering scars of my time with Camila and the Russians, it feels a little like the first time we stayed here, that first week of nothing but flirting and touching and making each other smile. And—I grab my plate before Dante can hand it to me—we have a deadline waiting for us in the city.

My semester starts in two more days. In New York City.

Neither of us are bringing it up. The one time I tried, Dante's whole demeanor shifted, and he said I needed at least three armed guards. I didn't even disagree, still don't, but the way he said it...I don't know.

There's something in the air now. Every time the Russians come up, Dante seems just on the right side of feral. And if I'm being completely honest, when I think about returning to the city, living in that apartment with or without Dante, nerves prickle up my spine. Camila escaped. Nobody has any idea who the Russians' boss is. Everything is different now.

Dante laughs so hard at one of the jokes he nearly dumps his pasta on the couch, startling me out of my thoughts.

"I told you it was good!" I say.

"Tell anyone about this and we're moving to Siberia," he replies.

I shake my head and open my mouth to tell him he'd look cute in a little fur hat, but his phone rings. Both of us freeze. It's either trouble in the city or Dr. Fletcher. After a second ring, Dante picks it up. I pause the movie.

"Uh-huh...Yes, I understand...That makes sense...Okay, thank you, Adelaide."

My heart leaps into my throat. Adelaide is the nurse who stuck around for the first day to help Dante take care of me. We're about to know, one way or the other. He hangs up and sets his phone in his lap.

"Just tell me," I rush out, my cheeks flaring with sudden heat. I don't know how I'm going to feel. Part of me is elated, ready, practically in pieces with excitement. Part of me feels nothing but gut-wrenching guilt for being so fucking irresponsible when so much is at risk right now.

"You're pregnant," Dante says softly.

I'm pregnant. My heart races. I put a hand on my stomach. Somewhere in there, a little baby is growing. A little baby endured the Russians with me. A little baby might have to go back to the city to get the computer engineering degree I've always dreamed of.

Dante doesn't say anything else. I don't know what to feel, what to think.

"Are you upset?" I ask.

"No." Dante sets his plate and mine on the table, then turns to me. His dark gaze is warm, inviting. "Never. Fuck, El, I'm thrilled. Having a family with you is a dream come true."

I run my thumb over his split cheek softly and study his face. His eyes pour love and belief into me, but I know him better than that by now. I can tell by the slight pinch in his eyebrows, the tiny downturn of his mouth, that he means what he's saying, he wants this, and he's just as terrified as I am about what this means.

"Okay." I nod. "Me too."

"Good." Dante sounds like he's trying not to pop the fragile balloon of hope between us. He grabs the plates from the table. "So then we'll finish dinner and have an early night."

I take mine and switch the movie back on.

WE'RE STILL MOVING around each other like the news of the baby is glass by the time we're getting ready for bed. We brush our teeth in quiet unison. Dante strips off most of his clothes and falls into the sheets in a pair of boxers. I change into one of his T-shirts from his football days, even bigger on me than most of his clothes, and a pair of clean panties. The wide, white bandage on my ribs crinkles slightly as I do. It's such a shallow cut that it feels silly to keep bandaging, but Adelaide was very specific. I crawl into bed next to him.

"I love you," I say, trying to put enough weight behind it to puncture the glass.

"I love you too." Dante smiles distantly and reaches for the light switch on his side of the bed. "Night, El."

The room goes dark. I lay on my back, fidgeting with the hem of my shirt. Dante flips one way, then the other, then turns his pillow over like it's already hot. I stare blankly at the ceiling, imagining the cracks from my cell.

"How are we going to keep a baby safe?" I blurt.

The glass shatters. Dante shuffles closer to me and wraps a gentle arm around my waist. "I don't know."

I swallow against sudden tears. It's not safe for us to have a family, no matter how much we want it. The smart move would be to get rid of the baby. But those words burn like what I can now confidently call morning sickness.

"How many kids would you want?" I whisper into the darkness instead.

Dante's answering chuckle is velvety. "Three. But I'd rather have more than less."

"Three is a lot to give birth to." I smile shakily. "It seems the first trimester doesn't agree with me."

He runs his hand over my stomach. "We can always adopt. Or foster. I just want a full house. Growing up an only child is very lonely."

I nod. "Siblings drive you insane, but it's nice not to be alone in the world."

Quiet falls. That distance threatens again. What he just mentioned is a silly dream. We can't adopt. We can't be foster parents.

We're in the fucking mafia.

"What if we ran away?" Dante murmurs against my neck.

My heart skips a beat. "Our whole lives are here."

"That's not true." He kisses my tender skin. "Mama's in Greece."

I laugh. "You want to go to Greece? We'd spend the rest of our lives fighting with Theia Adriani. She might be the worst boss of them all–"

"We have enough money, El." His kisses grow a little more insistent. "I could take both of you—all three of you away from Parikia. We'll go wherever there's a good engineering school."

Between his touch and the picture he's painting, it's impossible not to fall into him. "I'll transfer my credits from Tandon. But you and Mama will need something to do, so you'll open a restaurant."

I feel his smile against my neck. "Mama will cook. I'll run the numbers." He nips me softly. "You can waitress in your off hours, if you haven't lost the knack."

I swat him. "Why do you think we're having so many kids? We'll raise a gaggle of perfect servers."

He laughs, open and free. "And when you get your degree, you'll go get some fancy job that keeps the family restaurant afloat. I'll work part-time and take care of the kids the rest of the time." He ghosts a hand up over one of my breasts, and my body lights.

"It's perfect," I whisper.

1 0

PERFECT

Eleni

Over my clothes, under the blankets, Dante cups me like I'm made of glass. My thin shirt can't disguise the warmth of his skin, and though my whole body still aches, I want to tell him to treat me like normal. He thumbs over my nipple, and I arch up, tilting my head back toward the ceiling. In my mind's eye, I see the crack I tracked during the endless hours of my capture.

I shut my eyes. "Fuck me like you would if we were there."

"Quietly?" Dante's voice holds the ghost of a smile. "We have a lot of children and Mama not to wake up."

I picture a whitewashed house in Greece, next to the restaurant rather than on top of it, with a cozy front garden covered in plastic kids toys, far enough outside the city that I can commute and far enough away that the air tastes clean. A small grove of olive trees in the back where we picnic. I can almost taste the salt of the sea, just like Mama always described from home. In the darkness, it's easy to pretend we're already there.

"Yes," I murmur.

Dante's warm hand covers my mouth. He bends down to my ear. "Hush, love. I know we just moved the baby into the room next door, but the walls are thin."

I shudder, and warmth blooms in me like a flower. Our third baby, I decide. A boy after our twin girls. I nod against Dante's palm. The moon shining in through the window catches the edge of his smirk as he shimmies down the bed to press soft kisses to the skin of my neck.

"No marks," I hiss when he bites. "You know how Mama gets."

His laugh rumbles through my body. I relax into it. I'm home. Not just my home, my family's home. And we're all safe, at least for tonight.

Dante skims his hand up under my shirt, dancing around the thick bandage on my ribs. A cooking incident. I ran into a pan one of the girls forgot to turn in. He cups my breast, and the importance of the details fades. His thumb teases my nipple to attention in a few quick swipes. I pant against his hand on my mouth, harsh in the quiet night air. He stares at me for a few moments.

"You're so beautiful," he says.

"Even after the babies?" I ask through his makeshift gag.

"Even more so." He releases my mouth to pull my shirt up, over my shoulders, and presses the wad of fabric against my teeth. "Now shush."

I bite down on the cotton as he lowers his mouth to my chest. Here, he can leave as many marks as he wants, and he does, in spiraling patterns. I arch into him and let the T-shirt muffle my moans.

Dante takes his time with me, lingering on my breasts until I can feel the beginning of an orgasm curling my toes from that alone. Just as overstimulation threatens, he shoves the covers aside and yanks my panties down my legs. I don't need to look to know I'm completely bare before him now, hiding nothing in the soft moonlight. I don't need to check his face to see what he's thinking. I know him as well as I know myself by now.

Dante drags a line of kisses down my chest, along the length of my leg to my knee, and then back up the other side. I roll my hips, begging silently for attention where I need it. He presses his mouth ever so briefly on the hood of my clit, then rests his chin on my thigh.

"Are you sure?" he asks with a teasing smile. "I know you have your big meeting in the morning."

I very nearly spit out the gag to yell at him. Like he can see the thought on my face, his eyes darken with command.

"Fine," he says. "But we do this my way. Hands above your head, hold onto the bed. You let go or release the gag, I'll make sure the kids have a sleepover with the ill-behaved neighbor kids soon so I can give you the punishment you deserve."

My whole body flushes. I reach my hands up and grab the heavy wood posts of the headboard, then sink my teeth into the soaked cotton of the T-shirt. Dante palms one of my breasts before diving between my legs.

The first press of his tongue is like heaven. I've missed him painfully. He drags a line of wet heat along me, and I rock onto his mouth. Holding onto the bed instead of grabbing his hair burns, but my orgasm careens forward anyway. I love him so much I might explode.

He fucks two fingers into me, and I crash over the edge, trembling. Dante doesn't stop. He knows exactly what I can take. My second orgasm blends into the first, the shirt in my mouth valiantly trying to muffle my increasingly desperate noises. Dante laps up everything I have to give, and when he pulls back on the cusp of my third, the lower half of his face shines in the moonlight.

"Very good." He kisses my thigh and smiles. "Can you take more?"

I nod furiously. I could take a thousand orgasms if he wanted to give them to me.

"No, El." He ghosts a hand over my currently flat stomach, then grinds his stiff cock against my leg. "I mean *more*. Four kids sounds nice, doesn't it?"

A dam breaks in me, and hot tears pour from my eyes. Four kids sounds so ridiculously, beautifully goddamn nice. Four safe children, with his eyes or his hair or his way of commanding a room.

In a moment, Dante is back at the head of the bed with me, wiping my tears and trying to pry the gag from my mouth, but I can't let it go.

"I'm sorry," he murmurs. "Too far?"

I shake my head and finally convince my aching jaw to release the fabric. "No. Too perfect. I want it, Dante."

He smiles, but behind it I can see the same raw hunger consuming me. Dante wants four safe children.

"Some day." He kisses me.

I lean up into the kiss, catching his lower lip between my teeth.

"Tonight," I say seriously. "I want it tonight. Please."

He swallows and offers me the gag once more. "Tonight."

I accept the soaked T-shirt like a charm. Tonight, I'm Eleni Cattaneo, mother. Dante reaches over to the nightstand for a condom, and I release the headboard to grab his wrist. He looks at me for a long second, then smiles.

"Of course." He kisses the tip of my nose. "A condom won't help us tonight. But you did let go, so you'll be in trouble soon."

I laugh through the gag as he moves my hand back to the headboard. I can take anything he throws at me. After four children, even his harshest paddling doesn't hurt like it used to.

"Don't make fun of me." He sheds his boxers and takes his cock in hand. "I can always change my mind."

I shake my head furiously. I need him to fuck me.

"That's what I thought." He lines up with my entrance.

The sweet, bare friction of him almost makes me cry again from the sheer pleasure. Dante cups my face as he slides slowly home. He is beautiful too. I hope he finally knows it.

He fucks me slowly, inexorably, tracing circles over my clit in time with every thrust. He's dragging it out, gathering up the threads of my old orgasms and tying them into something spectacular. Warmth burns through me. I roll my hips against his, trying to coax him a little faster. Of course, he ignores me. Dante's dark gaze roves over my body, taking in every detail like he's worried he'll forget something. But he doesn't have to worry. We have forever to do this.

After long minutes, he murmurs, "Come for me, El."

We slide over the edge in unison, like slipping into a pool of warm water, brilliant and perfect and everything I wanted.

11

____

ROUND UP

Dante

Two days before El's first class at Tandon, Tony and I sit on the back porch of the safe house. I roll a glass of scotch between my palms and stare at the trees I know hide Christos' grave.

"I don't think there's another choice at this point," I say.

"She was just kidnapped, Dante." Tony takes a long pull of his beer. "Putting off college for a semester is a goddamn option."

I shake my head. "She'd be devastated. And she fucking earned it, Tone. I'm not letting Camila take this from her."

"And if you move her into the city, Camila only has the opportunity to take her life." Tony rolls his eyes.

I sip my scotch. He's been touchy since he found out about Henry. I know it's the right move. Even if it scares the shit out of me.

"Has there been more activity?" I ask. "Or are we just hiding from shadows at this point?"

"Nothing huge." Tony shakes his head. "I don't fucking know what they'd do at this point. They've got the drug trade in a stranglehold. Everyone's hiding from goddamn shadows at this point."

All of the Saints are still in hiding. Dozens are in Partridge with Mikey. More are just underground in the city. I stare back out at the invisible grave, and horrified realization crashes over me.

"We haven't buried Seb yet," I say.

Tony shakes his head. "Nonna and I did. Quiet. No funeral. She said she was going to kick my ass if we didn't."

He told Nonna. I said I would go with him when he did that. He fucking buried Seb. Fuck, I haven't even told Eleni. I've just let time disappear while we sit in the safe house, playing at being fucking safe. I've got a kid to take care of now, but I've abandoned everyone else who was depending on me.

"How are you?" I ask quietly.

Tony laughs. The sound is bitter, sharp-edged, and it slices right through me. My best fucking friend, and I've let him grieve his brother alone.

"I've been a shit," I say.

Tony raises his beer. "I'll drink to that."

I sip my own scotch. I tucked tail and ran when things got tough. The Saints have never fucking done that, and to have started under me is humiliating. So the Russians have the goddamn drug trade. Who gives a shit? We've never really bothered with that. So they've made some fucking waves. Nobody in history ever got anywhere rolling over and letting the bully have whatever they goddamn want. Cal Duncan might be a monster, but he's right, we can't just let the Russians wrap their tentacles around our goddamn city.

"I'm tired of hiding," I say.

"Took you fucking long enough," Tony mutters.

"Damn right it did." The criticism rolls easily off my back. I deserve it. "We can find a boss."

"Without the fucking feds?" Tony asks.

I swallow. I've made Henry certain promises. I might have enough on him to ruin his life, but mutually assured destruction doesn't appeal much more to me than sitting around in upstate New York for the rest of my goddamn life.

"As much as possible," I say.

"You shouldn't have brought them in." He shakes his head.

My temper flashes. Without them, Camila would still have Eleni. We didn't have a fucking lead in sight. But now's not the time to have this fight.

"I'm tired of fighting with you," I say.

Tony grunts in agreement. "Truce?"

"Fuck a truce." I set down my drink and stand. "I want a funeral."

He quirks an eyebrow.

"Seb's," I say. "And then the whole Russian fucking syndicate."

Tony knocks back the rest of his beer. "That, I can get on board with."

I pat my jacket for my gun out of habit and realize I'm unarmed. I have been almost the whole time El and I have been up here. How fucking cocky have I gotten? How far out of the game? I don't know how I'm going to keep my child safe, not yet, but I know that the boss of the Saints doesn't go down without a fight.

"Lou's," I say.

Tony nods. The little deli in the city is one of our best-kept secrets, hidden behind so many layers of shell companies Frank Lombardi didn't figure out it was mine when that was the heart of his territory. Now, with everything in shambles, nobody in the city is going to have a goddamn clue. Lou himself is one of those family friends that's related somewhere along the tree, just close enough to play the blood-is-thicker card when I need it. Maybe I'll even get El to toss a few extra protections on the place, however she does that.

"That's our headquarters, at least for now. Tell everyone to keep the comings and goings light, though." I pull in a deep breath. "I want everyone there. We'll have the funeral when we know everyone will be safe, but we need to talk. It's time to get back to work."

Tony stands. "Consider it done."

"And set up meetings with Cal and Wing." A little of my old energy starts coming back, infusing me with my old power. "They need to know."

Tony rolls his eyes when I say Cal, but he doesn't disagree. "So you're really coming back?"

I grin. "Come on. Did you really think I wouldn't?"

The split second of hesitation before Tony's "no" sends a shiver of something cold down my spine. I abandoned him, and he doubted me.

"Two days," I say with all the certainty I can muster. "Ready the apartment. Ready the guys."

Tony nods and heads off down the steps. I grab his empty bottle and the remains of my scotch, then head inside. El is upstairs, doing something. We still haven't really talked about a plan, just continued floating in the bliss of hoping something new might happen. It's stupid, looking back. Blissfully stupid, but stupid all the same. Both of us know avoiding danger doesn't make it go away. I toss Tony's bottle, finish my glass, and put it in the dishwasher. Even if domestic life is coming strangely easy to me. No, I have to go tell her it's time to face the music.

And exactly what facing the music meant for us last time.

12

FIDGETY

Eleni

I PACE back and forth in the guest bedroom we've set up as my kind-of office over the last few days. Dante got me a laptop, and Tony brought my school books on one of his many trips up here. I could study. Maybe I should be studying. Classes start in two days. But neither Dante or I have actually, seriously said we're going back to the city yet. I lift the blinds to check on him and Tony on the deck.

They're both gone. For a split second, cold fear grips my heart. The Russians found the safe house, and they took both of them while I stood up here. Any second now, the door to this room will burst in, and I'll be back in that fucking cell before I know it.

Someone knocks on the door, and my heart skips a beat. But Russians wouldn't knock. Dante would.

"Come in!" I say, hoping my voice doesn't sound panicky.

Dante opens the door and steps in. He looks taller, prouder than he did a minute ago. My battered heart leaps.

"What did Tony say? Good news?" I ask. "Russian syndicate destroyed-type news?"

Dante laughs. "Certainly not that good."

The laughter starts to soothe my fear, but then I hear the edge to it. Dante isn't just here to talk about nice things. I sit in the rolling chair behind my desk.

"What is it?"

He shakes his head. "I don't know how you know me so well already. Do you want the mixed news or the bad news first?"

I exhale slowly. Neither of those are good. "Mixed."

"We're leaving tomorrow." He leans against my desk. "Tony and I talked, and I realized that—while I'm so glad we stayed here while you recuperated—I can't just let the Russians run my city."

"That's not what Saints do." I offer him a wan smile. "So we're going back to the city to be mafiosos. I'll go to Tandon later."

I can live like that. Tandon was a pipe dream, if I'm being honest with myself. And as dangerous as this life is, it's more dangerous to leave enemies behind. For the next eight months, I have a baby to carry around and protect with everything I have.

Dante frowns. "Do you really think I'd just walk in here and tell you to give up your dreams?"

I bite my lip. "Not and expect me to roll over, no. But things are diff—"

He puts a soft finger to my lips. "You're going to Tandon. With guards. We're going back to the city to defend our life, our future, and you're not an incidental part of that, El."

My breath catches. I rub his wedding ring on my thumb, the cold reminder my ring is still lost at the bottom of the Hudson River. I need the guards. Not that guards stopped Luca Lombardi from trying to kidnap me during my final.

"One of them should be—"

"Undercover as a student?" Dante smiles. "Way ahead of you."

I kiss his finger against my mouth, and he withdraws it. Tandon. The baby and I are really going to college. Dante's willing to take on the whole Russian syndicate for that. Fuck it, I am too. I'm not just a piece of luggage he drags around. I'm a Staten Island Saint in my own goddamn right, and I know how to multitask.

"I still want to help with the business," I say.

"When you have time." He kisses my forehead and puts a hand on my stomach. "They need you healthy."

"They come first." I smile. "Can Seb be my undercover guard?"

He exhales slowly. "You remember the raid I went on, the night you got kidnapped?"

I nod. "Russians, right?"

"Exactly." He looks away from me, then back. "El, Seb took a bullet for me in there."

My blood roars in my ears. "So he's hurt? He can't come with me?"

Dante winces. "He died."

No. I heard him wrong. That just can't be right. There's no way I'm going to go back to the city, and Seb won't be waiting there for me with a hug and a smile. A stupid joke to make me laugh. Dante missed something because I haven't lost another fucking brother. I just haven't.

Sound filters back in. I realize I'm lying on the floor, having slipped out of my chair. Something is wet.

"...El." There's an edge of panic to Dante's voice. "El, you have to talk to me."

"No," I mumble.

He chuckles weakly. "You really hate orders."

I shake my head. "No. You're wrong. He's not—"

His blurry expression—the wetness is my tears—melts into something devastating. Something without a hint of confusion.

"I watched him die." Dante strokes hair back from my face. "Trust me, I fucking wish I was wrong."

I turn my head into Dante's lap and sob. My heart beats wet and ragged like someone tore it out. Not Seb. Never Seb. He was just about to become a capo.

"I know," Dante murmurs. "Trust me, I know."

"Wait." I whip my head to look at him. "That raid was weeks ago. Did I miss the funeral?"

Baba. Christos. I have never been allowed to bury someone I love.

"They interred him in the Bellini family plot, but we haven't had a proper funeral yet," Dante says.

Something hot and bright, a bit like the clarifying anger I remember in the wake of Baba's death, sears through my chest. "I'll plan it."

"What?"

I sit up. "I'm planning his funeral. I'll work with the capos, the mob wives, his nonna, hell, Tony, if I need to. But this is mine. You're not taking it from me."

Dante holds his hands up. "I'm not trying to. The funeral is yours."

I expect the bright feeling to burn out with the concession, but it doesn't fade. Seb needs this, and so do I.

"But...I have to ask." Dante strokes the naked place on my finger where my engagement ring used to sit. "Do you want out?"

"No." I bristle. "I just said that."

He shakes his head. "I mean...the boss of the Saints doesn't hide. But the boss of the Saints also loses a lot of people, loses them like this without time for a proper funeral." He meets my gaze, his dark eyes warm and uncertain. "I don't want you torn apart. Someone else could be the boss."

The imaginary salt air of Greece breaks over my tongue as the enormity of what he's promising yawns. He would actually run away with me, if I said the word. For me? For the baby? For himself? I don't know. For all of us, maybe. I cup my still-flat stomach. We could just be safe. We could leave this last fight to Tony or whoever else wants it.

That bright, flickering feeling calls my attention. Seb's funeral burns there, but so does my admission to Tandon, so do Mama and Baba's bright dreams of "making it" in America. My baby needs me. But maybe I need myself first.

"Not yet," I say.

13

APPREHENSION

ELENI

I SHUFFLE through the hangers in the walk-in closet attached to the bedroom in the city apartment Dante showed me just before everything went wrong a few weeks ago. Classes start tomorrow. Tomorrow! And I haven't even thought about what I'm going to wear yet. Most of my things from the house have been shipped here, but as I flick through them, all I can think about is how much longer they're going to fit me for. Leather pants? Silk camisoles? I couldn't have picked clothes with less stretch if I wanted to.

Someone leans on their horn outside, and I've lived here way too long to jump, but the city noises are still abrupt after so long away from them. The cell the Russians kept me in was almost completely silent, and there are no neighbors by the safe house. I missed the noise. I think.

My mind drifts to the house on Staten Island, apparently empty right now. It wasn't silent there by any means, just quieter. Quiet enough that I should've been able to hear the sirens headed for burning Piacere, if I'd been in the house when it happened. Yet another blow Dante's offered me in the past couple of days. I know he means well, and fuck, I don't really want to find out about this from anyone else, but we've lost so much.

I'm not thinking about Seb. I can't. Every time I do, I start to break down, which really isn't helping the funeral planning. Part of me just really wants to curl up in a ball in the bottom of the closet. The Eleni who ran the Saints is long gone, and I don't know where to find her right now.

Dante leans in the door. "I'm headed—oh, El." He crosses the room and wraps his arms around me.

I lean into his hug and try to draw strength. Dante's not falling apart. He's doing what needs to be done. Something jabs into my ribs. I pull back and look.

My stomach drops. Instead of his usual pistol, which I know how to hug around, Dante wears a bulky semi-auto that looks like it shoots .45s, if I'm seeing it correctly through his jacket.

"Where are you going tonight?" I ask through a suddenly dry mouth.

"Wing managed to put together a meeting with all the heads of the triads." He rubs my shoulders. "That's enough other players I wanted to be able to blow them away with one bullet."

I nod. He needs to re-establish the Saints. I know that. But a tiny heartbeat I'm sure I'm imagining in my stomach races every time I see him suited up with a gun in his holster.

"How late will you be?" I ask.

He kisses the side of my head. "I'll make sure I'm back in time to see you off tomorrow."

Too late for me to stay up. My sinking stomach drops even faster. It's got a whole skyscraper to descend through now.

"I love you," he says.

"We have to get me a new ring soon." I spin his on my thumb. "I don't like knowing I can't find you."

"Deal." He kisses me on the lips and walks out.

I stare at the rack of clothes in front of me, listening to his socked feet down the hall, then the sharp click of his shoes when he puts them on near the door. The door opens and closes, and he's gone. Just me and Matteo, the guard for the night. I sigh and push a few hangers around like that'll reveal what I want to wear.

The door opens and closes again. No gunfire. Probably Dante forgetting something. Then, footsteps pound down the hallway toward the bedroom. I rip open my underwear drawer and yank out the little six-shooter hidden within just as Gianna skids into view.

"Don't shoot!" She puts her hands up with a laugh.

I set the gun back down and take a few tentative steps toward her. "You're really here?"

"Yeah." She grins. "Did you really think I was going to let you live in a luxe downtown apartment without me?"

It's really her. I sprint the last few steps and throw my arms around her. I didn't even realize how much I missed her until she hugs me back. I've never had a best friend like her before. Suddenly, we're both laughing and crying and somebody started to sit so we're both toppling over.

"I can't believe you're really here," I say once we're lying awkwardly on the little couch in the middle of the walk-in.

"Me?" She pokes my arm. "I can't believe you're here. You went fucking missing, remember?"

"I can't forget." Silence falls for a moment, but I'm tired of silence. "What happened while I was gone?"

Gianna blows out a long breath. "Well, I'm out of a job."

Piacere burnt down. I nod.

"So I was thinking I might take my cues from you and go to night school." She offers me a sly smile. "Camila's a great reminder I can't dance forever."

That startles a laugh out of me. "What for?"

She shrugs. "Is there a way I can just try them all for a little?"

"Talk to Dante." I shake my head. "I've never gone to college with Saints money."

"Never yet." She shakes her head. "You start tomorrow, right?"

I groan. "Yes. That's why I'm in closet purgatory. I have no idea what to wear, and I just keep thinking about—"

Oh, fuck, has anyone told Gianna about the baby?

"About what?" she asks.

I put a hand on my stomach and try to find the words. Up at the safe house, a baby kind of started to make sense. Back here in the city? It barely feels real.

"I'm—"

"Oh my god!" She grabs my wrist. "For real? You and Dante?"

I'm so goddamn lucky to have a best friend who's basically a mind reader. "It's really early. Like, not even two months yet."

She covers her mouth. "I have to get rid of that champagne I brought. And has anyone checked the fridge for those soft cheeses Dante loves? They go to."

I laugh. "I don't think the fumes of either of those will hurt the baby."

"The baby." She melts. "I'm gonna be an aunt." She flicks her gaze up to me. "Right? Or a godmother or something?"

"I wouldn't dream of having it another way." I grin. "Now, please, help me pick out something to wear that'll survive morning sickness and Russian aggression?"

"You've come to the right woman." Gianna hops to her feet.

An hour later, the perfect outfit lies between half-full takeout containers of Chinese and a dozen discarded shoes. After all this time, it's so obvious I feel a little stupid. I'm not showing yet, and I need to feel good. So Gianna simply picked out the outfit we agreed upon so long ago, leather pants and all.

"You'll knock the nerds on their asses," she declares.

I take another bite of egg foo young and shake my head, but a little bead of excitement lights in my chest. I'm going to graduate, not just from some night school, but from one of the most prestigious engineering schools in the city. It's already a foregone conclusion. Between Dante and Gianna, I know I can do it.

She flops onto the bed in the other room. "You know how I mentioned Camila earlier?"

"Yeah." I join her with my legs crossed.

"Well, I actually know a couple people in the prison she got tossed in." Gianna twirls a curl of her dark hair. "No bail, RICO and conspiracy, by the way."

I nod. I knew she got picked up, but Tony never bothered to mention her charges.

"Do you want to hear something totally petty?" Gianna smiles.

I hate Camila like I've never hated anything. There's something about her that claws under my skin, ignites something worse than anger.

"Always," I say.

"She tried to 'establish herself' or whatever by taking on someone twice her size"—Gianna rolls over and meets my gaze—"but she's a goddamn dancer, so she got her ass handed to her!"

I laugh, remembering just how easy she was to fight after a week and a half in solitary confinement. In prison, Camila doesn't stand a chance.

Maybe I'd like to see that.

14

BLOW THEM AWAY

DANTE

"No," Wing says. "We're not getting involved."

I scowl at the four other half-lit men in the back of the mahjong house in Chinatown. "What, does he have you all by the balls?"

"No," another triad leader, Chan, replies. "We talked before you arrived. He speaks our consensus. It's too dangerous."

I turn to Tony, expecting him to be just as shocked as I am. The fucking triads, backing down? Tony looks back at me evenly. Fuck, he's right. I need to keep goddamn cool.

"What changed?" I ask.

Wing sighs. "The feds leave a wide trail."

I grimace. "Don't tell me this is about the deaths in Brighton."

"What else?" Chan slams his hand on the table. "Feds raid the Russians, get you your girl back, and who feels the pain? Russians. You know who will hurt if we help you?"

"The triads." Wing's voice holds an air of finality.

I shake my head. "They're eating into your territory, aren't they?"

"Territory can be recovered." Chan folds his arms. "Lives, not so much."

I stand. "Call me if you ever pull your heads out of your asses."

Tony and I stride out of the gambling den. Two days, I've been back in the city, and I don't have shit to show for it other than a meeting with my guys to make sure they're still mine. They are, thank God, but fuck. Didn't I used to make a difference?

"You get through to Cal?" I ask as we step outside.

Tony nods. "He sounded…enthusiastic. Said he'd meet us wherever."

That's almost worse than saying no. "McCreegan's. I'd rather know where the danger is."

We climb into the car. On the drive, my thoughts drift to Eleni, getting ready for her first day of classes. Gianna has to be there by now, hopefully keeping her from worrying too much. I wish I could be there. I wish I didn't have to run in at dawn to kiss her on the forehead before she runs out the door.

I wish I wasn't so fucking tired.

Tony parks the car in front of McCreegan's Pub, and we tolerate the dramatics of the through-the-freezer performance again.

"Some goddamn day, we'll walk into a room, and he'll just be there," Tony grumbles.

"Doubtful," I reply.

Cal pops up from behind the dark wood bar in the surprisingly busy secret pub. "Talking about me, lads?"

"Always," Tony deadpans. "You ready to meet?"

He smiles. "Drinks first."

And he pours three goddamn tankards of that awful beer. I am not in the mood for his antics tonight, but I have to be. So I let him lead us to a curtained-off booth in the corner and sit without a hint of the scowl clutched behind my teeth.

He raises his drink. "*Sláinte.*"

I knock my tankard against his and take a sip. It tastes like fucking dirt.

"So, Tony says you're looking to re-establish." Cal grins. "Trouble in paradise?"

"Not trouble." I lean back against the leather of the booth. It is comfortable. "Just coming out of hiding, looking to get our foot back in the door. Wanted to know where the Irish Kings stood on the Russian issue."

"We stand against the icy bastards," he declares. "What door? What foot? If you're interested in fighting the good fight, the Kings have all the resources you want." He pauses, slides his gaze over to me. "That is, unless your policy of no partnerships with yours truly still stands."

The sparkle in his eye tells me he already knows what's going to happen. I do too. So does Tony, by his scowl. The Saints survived underground, but we were far from thriving. I need to get us back into shape, making money, making changes. And that means I need to reform relationships we let lapse. Relationships someone like Cal may well have picked up.

Deep breath. El and the baby need this. It's the first step toward a safe future for all three of us.

"I've realized that policy was a little hasty," I say.

Cal crows in delight. "Saints and Kings, side by side? These streets'll run red with Russian blood by next Monday."

I put a hand up. "I have terms."

He tips his drink to me. "I would expect nothing less. State your demands."

I glance at Tony. We talked about this before I even asked him to call Cal. Despite his bitching, he agreed. But now he's slumped in the booth next to me like a moody teenager I dragged out to family dinner.

"Tony can tell you," I say.

Something hot and angry flashes in his ice-blue eyes. "Right. The Russians have snapped up the whole city center. All Lombardi's shit. The morsels of Coppola territory lying around. Chunks of your stuff, and the triads."

"Alas, I don't need the inventory." Cal takes a mournful drink. "I know it off by heart."

Tony rolls his eyes. "When this is done, we split it down the middle."

Cal hums. "Including that which my men have rightfully earned?"

"Given that we rightfully earned everything Lombardi and Coppola, yes," I reply.

He laughs. "Understood. Anything else?"

"We run this our way," Tony says. "No raids we don't know about. No half-cocked schemes. No sudden outside help."

Cal crosses himself solemnly. "Promise I won't take a piss without letting you boys know. Now, can we shake on it, or ought I get a Bible to swear over?"

Tony looks at me, irritation simmering in his eyes. I stick out my hand.

Half an hour later, after the celebratory drinks Cal insisted on, we walk out of the pub. I'm still humming *When the Saints Go Marching In*, which the rest of the Kings turned into a hell of a drinking song, and smiling. It's barely past three in the morning. I might get to wake up next to Eleni.

"You look like a kid who got a lollipop at the doctor." Tony opens the driver's side door and slides in.

I shrug and climb into the passenger's side. "I'm happy."

He drums his fingers on the wheel. "Is that because I'm about to take you back to her apartment?"

I look at him for a long moment. "Would that be so bad?"

He turns the car on and sits in silence. I watch him. She's what changed between us. Things have been off since I started falling for El, and I don't know how to fix it.

Tony glances at me. "I—"

My phone rings, and the car automatically picks it up.

"Cattaneo," Henry says.

Tony snaps his mouth shut, storm clouds roiling across his brow. Fuck.

"Alcott," I reply. "Late call. What's up?"

He sighs. "I need to talk to you. Now."

"Life-or-death now?" I ask tiredly.

"Damn near."

I look at Tony. Every muscle in his body is knotted.

"I'll see you soon." I hang up the call.

"I'm not going," Tony says as soon as it disconnects.

"I'm not asking you to," I reply. My night with Eleni slips through my fingers like a dream. "Will you drive, or should I take the fucking subway?"

Tony sits there for a long moment. I genuinely think he's going to tell me to get out and walk.

"Address?" he bites out.

Minutes later, we pull up outside the same diner.

"I'll wait," Tony says before I have to ask. "Text me a gun emoji if you want me to blow his fucking head off."

Catty Tony. Great. Exactly what I need right now. I adjust the oversized gun in my holster to be a little more subtle and get out of the car. Inside the diner, Henry sits alone in the same booth as last time.

"No Jace?" I ask as I join him.

"Not enough time." Henry frowns. "I already ordered coffee."

I nod. "That bad?"

He sighs. "I don't have full control over Camila."

My skin goes cold. "So the information she has is just out there?"

"Yes and no." He shakes his head. "She's not fucking talking, but when she does, it will be. Apparently, the white collar and public corruption guys have good goddamn reasons to want one of the first Russians we've picked up around here in almost a decade."

"That's what you get for playing tonsil-hockey with the government." I note the bags under his eyes, the wrinkles I swear weren't there last I saw him. Let him make threats. He looks like a suit on its third day of wear. "Bureaucracy fucks all. So, what do we do about it?"

"Can you talk to her?" he asks.

All my exhaustion burns away in one hot flash of rage when I picture Camila's face.

"That depends," I say quietly. "How upset would all those feds be if I murdered her?"

"Pissed enough to take it out on me for letting you in." He scrubs a hand over his face. "Fuck. Okay. What about your girl?"

15

A PART OF THE CROWD

Eleni

"How did you get the gradient?" Kaley leans over and points at the background of the webpage on my laptop. "I feel like CSS is organizing against me. I can't get it to work."

I glance at the front of the classroom, where Professor Villanueva taps away at her own computer. She said we weren't supposed to help each other with this assignment. It's a test of our initial capabilities. But then I look back at Kaley, who clasps her hands under her chin and flutters her eyelashes. God, she can't be twenty yet, can she? After my semesters at night school, I was able to start Tandon a little ahead of the usual freshmen, but Kaley seems so young.

Something in my stomach twinges. I swallow, praying it's not midafternoon sickness. Thankfully, the rush of saliva that always precedes my attacks doesn't appear. This twinge is more like what I imagine the baby kicking will feel like. When it can do that. Almost like the not-quite-baby inside me is telling me I should help out another at least relative baby in need. I sigh and lean over to Kaley's laptop.

"You haven't opened the supplementary image folder in the programming software." I open her file explorer and navigate through it quickly, glancing at the front of the room every few seconds just in case. Professor Villanueva is totally absorbed. I wish I knew what she's doing. From just her welcome speech alone, she seems brilliant. "Now try it."

Kaley reclaims her laptop and hits the button to rerun her code. The page loads with the soft blue to green gradient in the background.

"Yes!" She pumps her fist into the air.

A few other students turn and glare. I swallow my laughter as she flushes bright red and ducks behind her screen.

"Thanks," she mutters. "Your name is Eleni, right?"

I nod as I add a few more lines to my style sheet. Professor Villanueva wanted to see our very best landing page for a tech company, using the provided resources, and a landing page means there have to be buttons to navigate deeper into the website, even if I don't have content to put on them yet.

"I'm sorry if this is like, awful, but I haven't seen you around, and you're kind of...." She glances at me out of the corner of her eye. "Distinctive, I guess."

Does she mean my outfit? No one else is really wearing leather. There's actually a lot more cotton and sweatpants than I expected, just like at night school. Or—I look at her baby face again—does she mean I'm old? Next to Dante, twenty-four never feels like a big deal, but here, I look more like one of the professors than a student.

"I just transferred from community college," I say.

Her messy bun bobs with a nod. "Cool. My brother got an associate's degree. He said it was way more helpful for actually starting a career, but I had my heart set on this. Freshman year almost kicked my ass, not that I'd ever tell him that. Mom and Dad pinned all their hopes on me."

The little barb at the end stings, an unspoken agreement that a four-year university is better no matter what she says. All day, my classes have been like this. Academically challenging, full of fascinating professors I'd love to get to know, and what seem like literal teenagers who have no idea what to do with me.

Professor Villanueva stands up. "All right, that's our time for today. Email me your code—seriously, whatever you got done in class, because I'll be checking time stamps—and head out. Looking forward to seeing what you can do!"

The whole room fills with rustling as people pack up. I save my code in the editor, then in the version control system, then send it off to the email at the top of the syllabus from my new campus account. Kaley does the same, with a lot more fidgeting and cursing.

"I'm done for the day," she says. "Headed to Downstein before my homework crushes the will to live out of me. Hungry?"

Hunger these days is like a cat that really doesn't want to go to the vet. I have to sneak up on it, not make plans. And, more importantly, I didn't bother buying a meal plan since I was living off campus, so the dining hall is closed to me.

"Still have classes." I shrug my monogrammed leather messenger bag, a present from Dante to apologize for his absence this morning, onto my shoulder and smile. "Maybe next time."

She nods. "Totally!"

I jet into the hall ahead of her and turn deeper into the glass-walled building. Armando, my undercover guard, slices through the crowd after me. If I'm remembering the map I memorized correctly, there is an elevator that'll take me out this way. The other two guards will catch up.

Someone wolf-whistles. I make the mistake of looking up to see a cluster of guys in low-slung sweatpants staring at me.

"Nobody told me we got dancers this year!" one of them crows.

"How much for a private room?" another asks.

I flip them off and walk a little faster. The outfit was a total mistake. Less than half the guys I've talked to today have even acknowledged when I said I was a student. It doesn't feel like when Frank used to leer at me—I know I'm hot, and even better, I know all I need is a dark alley and a little luck to make sure they don't say shit to anyone ever again—but it is…I don't know, alienating? Just another reminder I'm not like the rest of the trust fund kids in here. It really is a good school. The professors have been incredible, and when people shut up and think, they come up with the kind of ideas I just want to turn around in my mind for hours. But between the wall of on-campus jargon, the constant references to moms and dads putting all their eggs in the kid's basket, and the three times I've had to run to the bathroom to throw up, it's hard to feel like I belong here.

Maybe it's the baby. I run a hand over my silk-covered stomach. The other students aren't that much younger, they're just more care-free. They can party all weekend and roll into class hungover. I have to worry about protecting a life. Several lives, if I consider the Saints.

I round a corner to see an elevator and allow myself a little happy dance in the relatively private hallway. Armando smiles.

"Long day?"

I heft my bag full of homework. "Not yet, but it's about to be."

He hits the button to call the elevator, and we wait as the other two guards, Leo and Dice, join us. A student turns into the little vestibule, takes one look at Leo's and Dice's suits, and turns back around. Just another thing to make me stand out.

The whole trip home is quiet as I turn over the day in my mind. I already have ideas about my homework, but part of me kind of wishes I wasn't going back tomorrow. I don't want to be stared at again.

At the top of the apartment building, the elevator doors *ding* and open to reveal Dante, wearing the same suit he left in last night. Still, I can't help smiling. It's been too long.

"Hey—"

"Don't get out." He hands one of my guards a backpack. "You have to go see an old friend."

16

MAKE IT HAPPEN

ELENI

I FIDGET with the waistband of the leggings Dante packed in the bag for me to change into before entering the prison and wish they hadn't taken my ring. Apparently, the whole "no metal allowed" thing isn't really negotiable. A burly woman stands on the opposite side of the table from me, one hand on her thick baton and the other on a walkie-talkie. I clear my throat.

"Vanessa?"

She quirks an eyebrow at me.

"Hank sent me." I feel ridiculous. All these code words…it's like I'm in a kid's movie, not a women's prison upstate.

Still, that makes Vanessa hit something on her walkie that dims the constant static pouring from it a second before the door buzzes loudly. I look up.

Escorted by two more guards, chained wrist to wrist and ankle to ankle, Camila stumbles in through the heavy door. She's barely recognizable. Her long, beautiful hair shines with grease in its loose bun at the back of her neck. The orange jumpsuit does the opposite of her

73

endless whites and pastels, turning her abruptly mundane under the fluorescents. A massive bruise purples half her face, barely starting to go green at the edges. Recent. I start to smile.

She meets my gaze as she throws herself into the chair across from me, and I see something wild in her eyes. Half feral. She sneers as the two guards who walked her in chain her to the table. She's putting on a show, trying not to seem weak. Or trying to make me think that. For all that I know I can take her in a fight, especially now that I have some sunlight and calories in me, but I'm not stupid enough to underestimate her.

The other two guards leave, and Vanessa leans casually against the wall.

"You're the last person I expected," Camila says. "I never thought you'd let me get within twenty feet of you again."

I cross my arms, half just to show off that I can. "And after this, you won't. But you have something that I need."

She throws back her head and laughs. Even that seems less special in here, more like a glass falling down the stairs than a chorus of glass bells.

"Everybody comes crawling back." She grins at me. "Finally realized I was right? That there's no life for women if we look out for anyone other than ourselves?"

For a split second, that almost makes me feel bad for her. I'm surrounded by more people to care about than I can count. Then, I remember what an awful bitch she is.

"Makeup tips, actually." I gesture to the side of my face that mirrors her bruise. "The colors are so dramatic. Who did that for you?"

She spits. "Ask me what the fuck you want to ask me and get out."

"I want the name of your boss." I smile. "Vanessa here'll get you some paper if you can't pronounce it."

She shakes her head. "Are you fucking stupid? That name is the only thing keeping me alive in here."

I stare at her for a long moment, anger roiling through my gut. She kidnapped me, locked me in a cell, starved me knowing I was pregnant, all because I dated her ex. She deserves everything that comes to her here. The cold Eleni who ran the Saints reaches out a hand for me, an offer of help, and I accept it gladly.

"From one point of view," I say. "From another, it would be very easy for me to place a few calls and kill you for pissing me off."

She pales to an unpleasant yellow color. "I'm not a snitch. Don't kill me just for having a code."

"I've got bigger things to fight for than a fucking code," I hiss. "There are lives on the line. And you might not be a snitch, but you're a fucking rat. That news alone could get you killed in here, even if I didn't bring down the whole wrath of the Saints on your pretty little head."

"The feds will protect me," she says, looking desperate. "They need me."

"Hey, Vanessa," I look up at the guard, "who do you work for?"

She grunts. "Special Agent Henry Alcott."

The fight drains out of Camila, leaving her even more of a husk than she was when she walked in. Even that feral light is gone.

"Fyodor," she whispers. "I don't think it's his real name, but that's what everyone calls him."

On impulse, I pat her head like a dog. "Thank you for your help. I'll be going now."

"Wait!" She shoots up. "You have to promise. Promise I'll be safe. Dante would want me—"

I stand. "Send her back to her cell, Vanessa."

Camila's shouts chase me out of the room and down the hall. The echoes ring in my ears as I take my things back. My phone lays heavy in my hand. It really would be so easy.

On the short walk across the parking lot to the car Armando waits in, I dial Gianna.

"How'd it go?" she asks.

"Make it happen," I reply.

～

DANTE IS GONE before I get back to the apartment. A note on the counter promises he believes I'm going to get everything we need out of Camila, but that he couldn't stick around because something came up with Piacere. And I shouldn't text or call him with anything I did find out, in case we're tapped or bugged. I sigh and show the note to Armando.

He shrugs. "Bosses are always getting called away."

I can't disagree with that, but the empty apartment does dim a little of my victory. I'm tired after a long day at school, and my thoughts drift insistently toward the huge bathtub.

"Order something for dinner," I tell Armando. "I'm not picky." My stomach rumbles. "As long as there's no fish anywhere near the meal."

He nods, and I wander deeper into the apartment. As soon as I'm sure I'm out of view, I put a hand on my stomach.

"Made the world a little safer for you today," I whisper.

17

IMPRESSIVE

Dante

I LEAN against the wall of the elevator chugging up the building to where Eleni waits and look at myself in the shiny black reflection. My suit nearly disappears, but my face sticks out like a sore thumb. If elevator reflections can be believed, I look pale and tired. In its defense, I feel pale and tired. It's Friday, and I've barely seen El all week except to pack her off to the women's prison to talk to a psychopath who kidnapped her. Even worse, I've spent almost the whole week at Piacere.

Just thinking about my once-beautiful club hurts. My shoes and the bottoms of my pants are gray from tramping through ash, trying to find anything in the wreckage worth salvaging. Somebody located the door to the basement, which is mostly untouched, on Wednesday, so we've been in and out of there constantly. I've got a metric fuck-ton of booze and nowhere to sell it. The stage, the lights, the bars, all gone in one blaze. Two people fucking died. Going out to Piacere every day is a nightmare, but I can't pick the business back up without it. Lou's has been a good interim headquarters, but it's fucking tiny, and I think Lou's about two snarky comments away from smacking Tony upside the head. No, we need Piacere or something like it, and that means figuring out what to do with what remains of the Russian attack.

The elevator dings, and the doors open into the apartment. One of Eleni's guards, Sal, looks up from his spot in full view of the door.

"Afternoon," he says. "She's in the office."

I nod gratefully and head that way, loosening my tie as I go. Before long, I start to hear voices. No, voice. Just El.

"Yeah?" she says. "What are the papers saying?"

That sounds like a school call. I slow down a little, trying not to interrupt.

"Mysterious." She laughs. "I like that."

There's an edge to her laugh I usually don't hear when she's talking about school stuff. I furrow my eyebrows and knock on the slightly open door to her office.

"What's up, Sal?" she calls.

I poke my head in. "Close, but no cigar."

"Dante!" She nearly throws her phone down, then seems to remember she's on a call. "Talk later. Bye." She hangs up and leaps out of her chair.

I step in fully and open my arms. She slams into me. I take a long, deep inhale. I've even missed the smell of her. Technically, we've shared the bed for at least part of most nights, but it's not enough. I need to see her more.

She pulls back first. "I didn't know you were going to be home on time today."

"Me neither," I admit. "But I was staring at this fucking spreadsheet, and I just thought to myself, what the fuck am I doing? I don't have to put up with this. I'm the goddamn boss."

She laughs. "I wish I could say that to my professors."

I groan. "That bad already?"

"No, not really." She circles back to her desk. "I was just trying to join in the complaining. Classes are actually going pretty well."

"Oh yeah?" I take the seat across the desk from her. "Well, I'm here now. Tell me everything."

She purses her lips and sits. "I'd actually rather tell you about Camila."

I'd rather never talk about Camila again, but how busy I've been all week does mean I have no idea how that talk went. Henry's been breathing down my neck for results. I gesture for her to continue.

"I got the name." She grins hungrily. "She doesn't know if it's his real name, but it's an interior one for more than just her. Fyodor."

"Fyodor." I roll it around in my mouth. "I haven't heard that before, but it's distinctive. We should be able to get some traction off it."

She juts her chin out proudly. "That's what I figured. And I've been very careful about using it. I don't want him to spook."

"Smart." I reach across the desk and take her hand. "Now can I ask about school?"

"One more thing." Her smile turns dark. "She's dead."

I blink. Camila, dead? I'd have heard about that.

She taps her phone. "That was Gianna with the news."

"How did it—"

My phone rings. I answer it quickly.

"She's fucking dead!" Henry hollers in my ear. "A goddamn heart attack, like I believe that. How did you do this? *Why* did you do this, after I told—"

I hang up the call. "I believe you."

She laughs, looking light and powerful and free. I study her for a moment. There's only one reason Gianna would've gotten the news first.

My phone rings again. Not Henry, so I answer.

"I'm sure you've heard," Lucio Mazzi, Ben's father and one of my newest capos, says.

"About the wicked witch? I have." I don't look away from El. "Why are you calling?"

"Because I've got an old enemy in that prison from my days with Thano, and I want to know how Eleni did it," he replies.

"I'll get back to you." I hang up again. "You did this."

She shrugs, and her oversized T-shirt falls off her shoulder, revealing she isn't wearing a bra. The knife-edged hunger around her mouth is intoxicating. The feds were breaking the rules, holding Camila in supermax pretrial. It should have been impossible to get anyone inside, much less to do so and kill someone as subtly as a false heart attack. Shivs are easy. Syringes, less so. It's damned impressive.

"You did it behind my back." I stand, letting an ounce of control bleed into my voice.

Eleni leans back in her chair to hold my gaze. "What if I did?"

"She was useful." I circle around the desk.

El doesn't flinch. "She was dangerous, and you know it."

"How healed are you?"

Her answering smile is a challenge. "As much as I need to be."

18

WITHOUT ME

ELENI

DANTE STARES DOWN AT ME, his black eyes burning. A laugh bubbles in my chest. Camila is dead. She can never touch either of us or the baby again.

"Did I ask you to kill her?" he says quietly.

If I didn't know him well enough to recognize the lilt of play in his voice even when he's pretending to be exactly the mafia boss I met so long ago, I'd be frightened. Instead, I smile.

"Did you ask me to go to the bathroom this morning?"

He grabs my chin hard. "It seems I've been a bit lax in your training, pet. You're acting out."

"I'm protecting this family." I run my tongue over the tip of his thumb. "When you couldn't."

He knows I don't believe that, but I watch doubt flicker in his eyes for a second. His grip loosens.

"Green?" I whisper.

"Are you just trying to rile me up?" he replies.

I nod. "I love you."

"I love you too." He kisses the top of my head. "Green."

His hold on me tightens again as he snaps back into his persona. "I am more than happy to remind you what happens when you try to do things without me."

I grin. "Do your worst."

"On the desk."

"This room isn't soundproof." I obey anyway, wishing I'd known he was coming and I could've changed out of the basic yoga pants I was wearing around the house.

He rips my shirt up over my head, exposing my bare breasts. "You think I don't know that? I'll fuck you in the middle of the goddamn living room if I want to. You're mine."

I swallow. The soft haze of submission welcomes me. "Yes, sir."

"Better." He twists one of my nipples roughly, and I barely stifle my cry. He scowls and does it again. "I want to hear you, pet."

I let the yelp escape, my cheeks burning. I have to spend every day with these guards. He smiles dangerously and takes his hand off me.

"Touch yourself."

I shove my hand into my pants and into the wetness already gathering at my entrance. My clit stiffens at the first touch, and I close my eyes on a gasp.

"Look at me," he snaps.

I open my eyes again. His gaze is hard, analytical, unavoidable. Even with my pants still on, I feel stripped bare for him. Soft moans tumble past my lips as I approach the edge of orgasm from his gaze alone.

Dante grabs my wrist and yanks my hand away. I groan and rock against the desktop at its absence.

"You don't come without me," he growls. Then, he releases my wrist.

Tentatively, I reach for the waistband of my pants again. He doesn't stop me. I return my hand to the warm wetness and my near orgasm. But as I approach the edge again, he grabs me once more.

"What did I say, pet?" He stares at me like he's already given me all the information I need. "You think you're so smart? Prove it. Follow a simple instruction."

My brain melted as soon as he took my shirt off. He can't really expect me to think now. But the merciless edge to his smile tells me he very much does.

Fuck it. I stuff his hand in my pants, and he traces familiar patterns over my clit. With a moan, I rock into his hand. He plunges two fingers into me and lets me fuck myself against his palm. Once again, I can see the edge. A tantalizing wave of pleasure is within reach.

He pulls his hand away. The whine that leaves me sounds barely human. He laughs.

"I thought you were a genius, pet." He strokes my cheek, smearing wetness across me. "My little engineer can't figure this out?"

I suck his thumb into my mouth and bob back and forth on it, trying to force my empty brain to think. Can't come without him. Can't come...without him!

His thumb leaves my mouth with a trail of saliva as I climb down off the desk, strip off my pants to reveal I also skipped underwear today, and reach for his waistband. He's already hard, and the zipper struggles along its track, but I force it. His cock springs free, and I start to straddle his lap.

Dante twists my nipple painfully again. "I said on the desk, pet. Or are two instructions too much for you?"

I shake my head and scramble back onto the desk. Now bare, I can feel my wetness smear on the glass. "Will you stand?"

He smiles. "Now, we're getting somewhere. Where do you want me?"

"Wherev—"

He slaps one of my breasts. "Answer the question."

"My pussy," I say. "Please, sir."

"Better." He pats my reddened skin and stands. "Do you think you can hold off if I fuck you?"

I nod. I need him inside me.

He grabs my chin. "The truth, pet. If I put my cock inside you, are you going to come before me like a greedy little slut?"

Wetness dribbles down my thighs. My core pulses with want, hungry and desperate. I drop my gaze.

"Yes, sir, I am."

"Good girl," he says. "Now lay down so I can fuck your pretty little mouth until I'm good and ready."

I spread myself across my desk, pushing pens and schoolbooks out of the way heedlessly. Dante comes first right now. He spanks my ass, seemingly just for fun, then pushes my legs apart. If anyone came in right now, they'd see every inch of me from the second they opened the door. I shudder and open my mouth.

Dante slides his cock past my lips like he's coming home. I moan at the salty taste of him. It's been far too long. He takes a deep breath and smiles like he's thinking the same thing, then fists a hand in my hair and begins fucking my mouth. Tears and drool blend on my cheeks. I relax my throat, accepting more and more of him. His aggressive thrusts push me across the desk.

Abruptly, I realize the edge has lined up with my clit, and if I roll my hips just right, it provides blissful friction. I grind subtly against the desk, chasing his orgasm and mine. Dante never needs to know.

I careen over the edge with a moan that verges on a scream. Before I'm finished shaking, Dante rips me off his cock by my hair.

"I thought I was very clear," he says. "You don't come without me."

I writhe in his grasp, barely human in an ocean of pleasure. "I-I thought I was clear. I was right."

"You're such a brat," he snarls.

I can see the sparkle of laughter, of celebration in his eyes.

"Don't you want to fuck me anyway?" I pant.

He sits back down, drags me onto his lap, and impales me on his cock.

"Impossible." He buries his face in my bouncing breasts. "Never going to learn."

"No, I'm not." My next orgasm is already a promise on the back of my tongue. I plaster myself against him, trying to ruin his perfect suit with my mess. I love Dante. I can't imagine a life without him. But I'm not taking reprimands today.

He stiffens with a groan, and I ride him a few moments longer, until my own orgasm washes me away.

19

—————

CAUGHT

ELENI

"THANK YOU," Mikey, one of Dante's older capos, says in his gravelly voice. "I know Dante's been pulling things together for a couple weeks now, but it didn't feel right starting things up again without toasting the kid."

I swallow against a lump in my throat and glance at one of the pictures of Seb hung in the room. "I know what you mean. And thank you for your help out here."

He raises a glass. "Hey, I'll take the credit, but most of it belongs to my Adrianna."

His wife, a slightly tidier version of the mafia wives I've grown used to in Staten Island, smiles. "Don't let Mikey trick you. He strong-armed the owner into letting us have the place on such short notice."

I raise an eyebrow. The quiet event space over the bridge in Partridge is perfect, close enough to the city to get back if something happens but far enough that we all agreed the Russians wouldn't try to crash. That said, I'm not sure I want someone strong-armed into it.

"Adri!" He laughs. "I promised to coach softball this season. She just likes making me seem like the bad guy."

I laugh with them, but something in my chest aches. The pair of them move together so easily. We're all at the same funeral for Seb, but they have concerns like softball and who gets to aim their stories. Over these past couple of weeks, I've realized I can't talk to Mikey or Adrianna long without my chest hurting. I offer a few quick goodbyes and drift off into the crowd.

Clusters of black-clad mobsters studs the open event space. The high ceiling bounces back strained laughter and orders for drinks. Everywhere I turn, there's a picture of Seb's face, or someone I half-recognize telling a story about him. Tony holds court in one corner, Dante at his side for once and his nonna at the other. The little old woman had strong opinions on the funeral, even though she couldn't get out of her apartment to come to any of the meetings, but the moment I saw her today, she threw her arms around me. Waves of grief roll through the space, but most faces hold wan smiles. Would Seb have liked this? I want to think so, but surrounded by these people who have known him for so long, I can't escape the fact that I really only knew him for a few months. I've told all my stories already.

I find myself face to face with a picture of Seb, a candid shot with his head thrown back in laughter. Tears pinch the corners of my eyes. I should be thinking about him right now, but I keep thinking about all the family I've lost.

"I want to say you would've liked Christos," I tell the picture. "But I don't think that's true. He would've made fun of you with Tony, and then Tony would've tried to knock his teeth in because only Tony can talk about you like that."

It's easy to imagine his golden laughter pouring out of his mouth.

"But I wish you'd met," I continue. "My brothers. Both of you."

A few tears spill as a hand lands on my shoulder. I turn, hoping for Dante but knowing he won't leave Tony unless something's wrong. The hand belongs to Nicky, resplendent in a black and gray Chanel skirt-suit and surrounded by a passel of other mob wives, as well as Chloe.

"You two got pretty close, huh?" she asks.

I swipe away my tears with a laugh. "I needed a lot of body-guarding over these past few months."

A chuckle ripples through the crowd of women. This, they understand. I resent them all a little less now. They really have been great about helping me plan this funeral.

"Well, you're Italian now, and we feed grief. Have you eaten?" she asks.

I shake my head and don't tell her Greeks do the same, I just haven't had time. Nicky snaps, and a plate floats forward along a sea of hands.

"Here." She offers it to me. "Some bread, some pasta, a little bruschetta."

I reach to take it with a smile, but then the smell of the bruschetta hits me. The vinegar twists my stomach with an iron fist. Oh, fuck.

"Um." I swallow against the saliva filling my mouth. "I actually have to go wash my hands first."

I turn and hurry away, hoping that looked normal. The women's room has a line at the door, but I remember the tour Adri gave me earlier. There's a single bathroom for the owner in the back. I veer out of the main event space, slam open the office door, and land on my knees in front of the toilet a few seconds before my breakfast comes back up.

Fucking morning sickness. I slump over the ceramic, panting and hot. It has the worst goddamn timing.

Someone knocks softly on the office door, and I don't have the energy to answer. The door opens. Once again, I mentally cross my fingers for Dante.

I'm actually not expecting Chloe. Her blonde hair hangs loosely around her shoulders, and she looks at me with an expression thankfully far closer to worry than pity. Without a word, she runs the sink behind me, then crouches at my side with a cold, wet washcloth.

"Mom thought you were avoiding her," she says, "but I saw you turn green."

I laugh wryly. "Me? Green?"

Chloe dabs my forehead with the cloth. "You're pregnant, aren't you?"

My empty stomach crunches in on itself. Dante and I agreed. We couldn't tell anyone. It was way too dangerous.

"I'm not… not trying to imply anything." She wipes a little more sweat away. "Congratulations, and I'm sorry. I know how scary this probably is. Does he know?"

I blink a few times and peer at Chloe. She really doesn't seem like she has a mean bone in her body, and the way she said she knows…I trust her. Maybe that's stupid, but I need to trust someone other than Dante.

"He does," I say. "But…pretty much just him."

"Not even your mom?" she asks quietly.

Tears sheet down my face, quiet and lonely, as I shake my head. An international call is easier to break into than a local one, with the encryption software we have. It just isn't safe. And Mama will be so upset I'm pregnant before I'm married, with me and with Dante.

Chloe makes a soft sound in the back of her throat and wraps her arms around my shoulders. "I promise, she's going to be less mad than you think. Really. I met your mom when she was in town, and she loves you so much. That's all that's going to matter."

We sit there like that for a long, quiet moment.

"People are going to start asking questions," she says finally. "Let's get you cleaned up."

I nod. Chloe is nothing like Gianna, who would flutter wildly around me, talking and explaining. Instead, she helps quietly, filling in the steps in the process I miss or don't think of without a word. She doesn't need to ask. Part of me wonders how much those pale eyes of hers see, standing quietly in her mother's shadow. But after a few minutes, I look presentable once more. Chloe squeezes my hand once.

"Just another hour," she says. "Then, go home and call your mom."

I nod. Together, we walk back out to the main event space. Across the room, Dante catches my eye, and his brow furrows. I shoot him a quick smile, a promise there's no disaster. But I'm not completely sure. Chloe is the first person outside our inner circle to know. How much longer can we keep this up?

20

FORK IN THE ROAD

ELENI

AFTER THE FUNERAL, Dante is quiet in the car. The windshield wipers fill the silence between us as we sit in traffic, headed back into the city.

"Do you want to see Piacere?" he asks suddenly.

I pluck at the hem of my dress. My stomach is still empty, grumbling in a way I know means I'm losing the next thing I put into it too, and I'm exhausted. But the club I spent so much time in this summer, the place Dante and I really met, is gone, and I haven't really internalized that yet. Today seems like a day of saying goodbye to things. The secret growing inside me. What Seb and I could have been to each other, if only we had the time. I may as well look at the remains of the life I thought I was going to have when I entered Piacere that first night.

"Yeah."

He twists the wheel, and we pull out of the traffic headed into Manhattan for the slightly lighter traffic aimed at our island. The long silence of the drive is almost meditative. Snippets of the last few months slide through my mind. I've been so many versions of myself that the waitress I started the summer as wouldn't recognize me anymore. I don't know if I'd recognize her either.

I glance at Dante and wonder if he feels the same. His all-black suit looks like the one he wore in the Greek Corner. But the lines around his mouth, the exhaustion in his eyes, those are new. So is the warmth when he catches my gaze.

"Penny for your thoughts?" he says.

"Just thinking about how much has changed." I run my hand over my stomach.

He places his warm palm over mine. "I've been spending a lot of time doing that lately."

The car pulls onto the street Piacere used to dominate. Among the lineup of other clubs, its absence is sickening, like a pulled tooth. My stomach churns as Dante pulls to a stop. The soft rain spits down on the car and the grayish sludge that used to be the most popular dance spot on the block. I exhale shakily.

"Wow."

He nods. "I didn't expect it to be this destroyed the first time either."

"It's just…gone." I blink back more tears. I've been crying so much lately. Let the sky do it for me, at least for a little.

Dante folds his hand around mine and stares out the window. "You know, my father built Piacere. I remodeled the place, made it my own, but the structure was his."

"Baba bought the Greek Corner," I say, not knowing what else to add. "He always wanted to expand. Sometimes, I'd find him and Mama talking about what they would do if they could build something new."

Quiet enfolds us. I picture the Greek Corner like this with the same pulled-tooth sickness. I haven't been back there in so long.

"I don't know if I'm going to rebuild," Dante says abruptly.

I blink. "What? I thought you just got the insurance check."

"I did." He exhales slowly. "And I gave every penny to the families of the people who died in the fire, or those who were injured but survived. Seb's funeral wiped out the last of it."

The announcement rings hollowly through my chest. Dante has money, I know. More than enough to rebuild Piacere, or build somewhere new. But suddenly, I don't want to be talking about building a club I can't drink in. I want to strong-arm our neighbors by offering to coach the softball team.

"Are you happy?" I ask. There are no other words big enough to encompass the feeling threatening to swallow me whole.

Dante shuts off the car, silencing even the wipers. There's nothing but us, our not-so-steady breathing, and the rhythmic hum of the rain. A river of ash winds into the street, streaking grayly across the nearly black pavement. Finally, Dante squeezes my hand, and I think that's all the answer I need.

We don't belong here. Not anymore. I turn to Dante and open my mouth to ask him if he feels the same weight of...I don't know, destiny pushing us out of the life.

His phone rings. I can see the caller ID where it sits in the cupholder. Cal Duncan. A couple days ago, Dante gave him the name Fyodor, and he and Cal aren't exactly drinking buddies. The call can only mean one thing. After an interminable moment, Dante picks it up and hits the speaker.

"Cal," he says.

"Dante!" The lilting Irish brogue is butchered by the phone speakers, but I can picture his red hair and broad smile. "I was hoping I might've waited long enough for your little get-together to wrap up."

We didn't tell Cal about the funeral. Just another shred of privacy ripped away.

"What is it?" Dante asks tightly.

"I've got a lead on our mutual friend," Cal says. "And my trigger finger's getting out of practice. What if you muster up a few of your lads, and we go get back in shape?"

Dante stares at the phone, then looks up at me. His eyes are like black holes, but I know how to read between the lines. His mouth pulls down. He doesn't want this news now. His fingers clench around the screen. He wants to go. His gaze drops to my mouth for a second. He wants to stay. My chest cracks in two. If he goes now, this could be over. It could end in the September rain, and we could really talk about what our life looks like from here.

Or he could die. Cal could be wrong, or not careful, or just lying, and I could lose Dante. Every time he walks out the door, I could become a single mother. I don't know him well enough yet to know if he's thinking that.

"Use your home gym," Dante says. "We need to get all our buddies together before we check out any old friends."

Cal huffs. "I've never heard of Italians being over-careful. But I suppose it's your call. I'll keep my lads on ice."

Dante hangs up without another word.

"Take me home," I say.

He turns the car on. "The traffic into Manhattan is gonna be a bitch."

I put a hand on his arm. "Home, Dante. No traffic."

He smiles quietly and pulls into traffic, headed for the house on Staten Island.

2 1

HOME

Eleni

When Dante parks the car in the driveway of the house that changed my mind, which I now haven't seen in over a month, something in my ribcage snaps.

"I'm tired," I say.

He nods.

"I'm tired of being tired." I put my hand on his cheek.

With a sigh, Dante nods again.

"I'm twenty-four." My voice shakes. "You're thirty-three."

He laughs bitterly. "Who would believe that?"

"No one." I unbuckle my seatbelt. "And I'm tired of that too."

That seems to catch his attention. He looks me over, trying to figure out what's going on.

"Let's just be young tonight." I smile. "Let's... Let's streak through the neighborhood."

"I don't know that I'm willing to share like that." He chuckles. "But I don't think you've ever been in my pool."

My smile starts to grow. "Too busy all summer. But I don't have a swimsuit on."

He unfastens the button holding the front of my jacket together. "Who says you need one?"

The blazer falls open, displaying the modest black blouse underneath. I loosen his tie.

"I thought you didn't want to share."

"It's not that far to the backyard." He presses his lips to my neck, and the rest of the world fades away.

It's a good thing I can take his clothes off with my eyes closed at this point. He keeps my head bent back, sucking bruise after bruise into the tender skin of my neck, as we strip each other. The car AC makes my skin pimple with goosebumps, so I press myself closer to him, soaking up the warmth of his body. His chest hair scrapes over my nipples. I gasp as one bruise stings sharply.

"You… you usually don't mark me where people can see," I stutter.

"We're young, and our life is simple." He smiles against my skin. "What do I care?"

I laugh and struggle to pull his pants and underwear down between the seat and the wheel. With a few bumps and curses, we're naked, our clothes scattered over his car. I squeeze his hand.

"Race you?"

He laughs. "Good luck, pet."

My body flushes as I wrench back from him, open the door, and sprint into the warm summer rain before he can finish making fun of me. Sloshing and an echoing slam promise he's right behind me. My breasts bounce freely against my chest. His legs are so much longer than mine. I don't stand a chance, and I don't care.

I reach the gate to the pool a second after him, but he just wraps me in his arms and presses me against the metal. It's cool, the only thing keeping me from burning out of control between the rain and his body. He kisses me like the world is ending, like we'll never get another chance, and I press up into him. When he bites my lip, I bite his. When he sucks my tongue into his mouth, I do the same. He groans, and with a little metallic fumbling, opens the pool gate. I don't move. Dante smiles, cups my ass, and lifts me off the ground.

I wrap my legs around his waist and grind onto his stomach as he carries me inexorably toward the pool. The slosh of grass and mud turns into the slap of wet feet on concrete. Then, without releasing my mouth, he jumps, and we are airborne.

The splash is tremendous. I separate from him as the warm water envelops me, laughing in great bubbles of sound. All my aches fade as gravity lessens, and I feel immortal.

I surface to find Dante staring at me from the shallow end, the water barely lapping at the top of his cock. I paddle to stay afloat.

"Catch me if you can!" I smile and duck below the water again.

I learned to swim in the YMCA pool around the corner, swimming laps with a not-very-patient college student. I used to go there to relax in the summer, early in the morning or late at night when it wasn't too crowded. Here, I have the advantage. I hover in the water, waiting to feel the vibrations of his movement.

There. I dart through the water then catch him around the waist. We both surface, spluttering.

"I thought I was catching you," he said.

"I know." I kiss him, savoring the taste of chlorine and rain.

He kicks us slowly backward through the water until at least he can stand. I paddle, a little breathless, and he hooks my legs around his waist once more. That's not fair. I want him as much as I want to make him play. I grind against him, frictionless.

"Are you going to make me catch you again?" he murmurs.

"Forever," I reply.

There's a heartbeat where I could stay, could reposition his cock to fuck myself on it and let this end. But I want the endless summer I can taste on his lips for just a few moments longer. I release him and jet away toward a current of warmer water I think promises the attached hot tub. Even underwater, I can hear him laugh and call me a brat.

Warmer, warmer, hot. I surface and find myself surrounded by low, stone seats and bubbling water. Dante catches up a moment later.

"Pregnant women can't use hot tubs." He grasps my waist and lifts me out of the water to sit me on the side.

I pout. "No fun."

Dante raises an eyebrow, then pushes my legs apart and dives between them. I gasp and latch a hand in his wet hair. His tongue paints pictures on my pussy, teasing my clit, delving inside me for only a second at a time. I rock against his face until he puts a finger inside and turns his mouth's attention to my thighs, leaving another string of bruises along either side.

"Fuck me," I gasp.

"Say it louder." He fits another finger inside me. A pleasant stretch, but far short of what I need.

"Fuck me, sir," I moan.

A third finger. "Louder. Say my name."

"Dante!" I roll my hips, trying to draw him closer. "Fuck me, please."

He hums. "A little more, I think."

I grab at my breasts, pinch my own nipples, make a spectacle of myself. "Oh, fuck, Dante, I need your cock inside me."

"Good, pet." He raises out of the water and thrusts inside me in one smooth motion.

I nearly scream. Dante keeps moving, lifting me off the side of the pool, dropping me onto his cock as he walks. I abandon one of my breasts to lock an arm around his neck, holding on though I know he won't drop me. My orgasm builds, sloppy and desperate.

A blast of cold air hits my back. Dante opened the sliding glass door and carried me inside. As my moans grow in pitch, he continues through the living room, both of us dripping wet, and up the stairs. Finally, he lays me down in bed, our bed, and begins slamming his cock into me. My screams peak, and pleasure explodes through me.

When I start to come back down, he is softening inside me, but he hasn't left.

"I don't think you should've run away from me, pet," he says with a small smile. "What do you think?"

I grin. "I think I don't know what you're talking about, sir."

MAKING THE RIGHT CHOICE

Dante

Sunday morning comes bright and early to the bed I custom-ordered so long ago to hold the random women I was fucking. When I wake up next to a naked, fucked-out El, covered in bruises she begged me for from neck to knee, my first thought is that I've never asked her if the mattress is comfortable. She's going to be my wife, the mother of my children. So much of our life is still mine. I kiss her sleeping cheek and roll over to check my phone for mattresses that allow people to adjust both sides to their comfort.

I should've known. My screen is covered with notifications. Capos, allies, people from the funeral. Tony. I open his first.

Cal called me too. I set up a meeting with him and a triad representative to talk. I'll roll your ass out of bed if I have to.

I snort. Cal Duncan is getting bossy. But neither he nor Tony is wrong. If they really have a lead on Fyodor, I need to fucking do something about that. I roll out of bed with a groan and dress quickly to hide the marks El left on me as revenge. The rest of my notifications are less pressing. I flick through them while I make coffee, then write a note to El and leave it on the counter. By the time Tony texts that he's outside, I'm more or less ready to face the day. I pour another coffee for myself and one for Tony into to-go cups and stroll outside. He sits behind the wheel of his favorite car, looking tired. He was mostly quiet at the funeral yesterday, letting other people talk, and I wonder how he'll be today. The text suggests he's at least somewhat back to his old self.

Still, when I get in the car, he's silent for a long moment.

"Tell Eleni," he says slowly before pulling out, "thanks."

"You could do it yourself." I offer him his coffee.

He takes it, shakes his head, and begins the long drive into the city.

I sip my coffee, and instead of focusing on the important meeting waiting for me on the other end, my mind drifts to last night. El's right. Despite everything, we're somehow still young. At least, in theory. I don't know if I've been young since I graduated college, even before my dad died. But there was a freedom to last night that I've been missing. Pretending we had nothing to be scared of… it was damn near more fulfilling than pretending we already had the family we've been dreaming of.

"What do you think would happen if I didn't go to this meeting?" I ask.

Tony glances at me out of the corner of his eye. "I'd think you got out of bed for no good goddamn reason."

"No, I mean—" I shake my head. "Do you think you could handle it? Cal and Wing?"

He stares out the window at the city growing larger in the distance. "Cal's easy. A hell of a lot easier than he thinks he is, even. Wing…he wants to think of himself as the logical one. He loses respect for people who blow up, but he doesn't want to be outthought either." Tony shrugs. "It'd suck, today, but I think I could do it."

I nod slowly. I wouldn't have described Wing like that, but to be fair, I keep blowing up at him. The old triad liaison was easier to work with.

"Fuck, I'll say it." Tony sighs. "Your priorities have shifted. You're asking me how I'd handle things. Are you walking out?"

I swallow. Am I? Every time El and I approach the conversation, we back down again.

"Tell me before I have to pick up the pieces of a syndicate you disappeared on in the dead of night," Tony mutters.

"I'm not gonna do that to you," I say quickly.

"And the rest?"

I let the question hang in the air for long minutes.

"We have to handle the Russians first," I say. "Then, I'll take a good, hard look at my priorities. But you have to do that too. I'm not dropping something on the shoulders of a man who doesn't want it."

Tony nods, and we drive the rest of the way to the neutral meeting location he picked out, some bodega in Queens, in silence. When we arrive, the taciturn owner escorts us to a back room where Cal and Wing are already waiting with their own seconds.

"And here I thought we were going to have to meet without you," Cal says without heat. "That Verrazano giving you trouble?"

"Something like." Tony drops into one of the empty chairs around a circular table. "Let's be frank. The guy out front runs a floating card game. He's not loyal to us, but he's not loyal to *any of us*, capiche?"

Cal flips a salute.

Wing sighs. "Mr. Duncan was just about to tell me what he knows. Are you sure we're free from prying ears?"

"Prying ears who give a shit, yes." I sit next to Tony. "What do you have?"

Cal grins. "Fyodor isn't a name with a lot of personal buzz, but it opens a few doors, if you know where to give it out. I've got the bastard's network, or at least a chunk of it."

Wing sits forward. "Warehouses, runners, bases?"

"And all," Cal replies. "Though I figure each we hit'll unlock a few more."

I grin. "Sounds like it's time to smoke his ass out."

Wing puts up a hand. "Hold, gentlemen. You seem to have worked out some kind of agreement, and while I'd love the Russians out of the city as much as the next one, I don't intend to be left out of a territory agreement."

Cal laughs. "G'wan, there isn't an agreement here beyond returning what's properly ours."

"And the Lombardi territory?" Wing looks at me.

"Split between the Kings and the Saints." I cross my arms. "Because we dropped both Lombardis, if we're taking stock, and Cal tracked down this network. You bring together something this good and we'll talk."

"How does this appeal: we split it three ways, and I don't bring all of Chinatown down on your head?" Wing says.

I laugh tiredly. "We all have organizations to bring to bear. Any one of us hits one of the others, the other two pound him to dust."

"I will not be forgotten." Wing scowls.

An eye roll and the words, "couldn't if I tried" sit on the tip of my tongue, but I remember Tony's words in the car.

"There's a straight shot from Chinatown to the harbor through Lombardi territory," I say. "Free passage through there in perpetuity, no announcements needed."

"Now, that cuts a tail of Kings land," Cal complains.

I look at him. "I know. But the Russians are swarming this place like rats, killing our people and taking our shit. Together, we can crush them. Is a tail worth the whole goddamn rat king?"

Cal scowls. "Put your fellas in a color. I don't care what, but let me know so I don't take an innocent agreement as something untoward."

Wing inclines his head. "This, I can do. Shall we parcel up the work, then?"

23

DISTRACTED

I WAVE goodbye to Kaley and turn away from her after yet another class. We're...two weeks into the semester now? Three? No, Professor Villanueva was talking about midterms. How could so much time have passed already?

Armando walks up beside me. "Headed home?"

I shake my head. "Tony needs a little birdie, and it's easier to hide my traffic under the other students here."

"But—"

I put my hand up to silence him. "Just...let me have this, okay?"

Armando stuffs his hands in his pockets and nods. I veer away from the hall that takes us to the back elevators and toward one of the many computer labs. Not that I'd actually use a school machine. That's insane. But if I work on my laptop in the seating area right outside, it's easy to spoof one of the IPs in there and disappear into the flow.

That's really how these last god-knows-how-many weeks have felt. Disappearing into the flow. I bounce between Tandon and the apartment, juggling school work and Saints' work and morning sickness that shows no sign of abating. Every night, Dante or no, I drop into bed and fall right to sleep. If someone broke in, I'd be dead. Nothing wakes me up anymore.

As I set up in the armchair, a pang of guilt shoots through me. I should really try to be better about that. If I die, the baby dies. It just… still doesn't feel real. The pregnancy. Wearing sweatshirts and sweatpants to class makes it easier to blend in, and it's not like I'm the only sophomore running to the bathroom between classes to puke. I'm just not doing it because I spent my weekend at Rikki's kegger in SoHo.

Maybe that's why I still haven't called Mama. I know Chloe was right. I need her, and in the end, she's going to be so thrilled about a grandchild that everything else will fade away. But I don't feel like I need her for the pregnancy. I need her to hold me and tell me everything's all right, that I'm making the right choices. Whatever those are.

I push all the other concerns aside and log in. The Saints, together with the Kings and the triads, have been eliminating a string of Russian safe houses and warehouses one by one. My job is to bug and track Russian devices, everything from doorbells to tablets. Today, Tony gave me the chip from a car they're going to dump bodies in tonight, and he wants me to plant a listening device and tracker—something he's started calling little birdies, as in, a little birdie told me—on it before the Russians pick it back up. I slot the chip into my laptop and scan for viruses.

The work is easy at this point, nearly habitual. I crack the encryption, plant the bug, add a few flourishes I learned in another class to cover my tracks, and frown. The professor taught them to us in case we need to edit code we've already turned over to a client, said they were for emergencies only. This doesn't feel like an emergency.

I blink and sit back. Who have I become that a car with four bodies in the middle of a gang war isn't an emergency?

Before I can answer that question, my phone rings. Dante. I pick it up.

"Hello?"

"El?" His voice sounds tight. "Where are you? Are you okay?"

I close up my code editor and eject the chip. "Uh, I'm at school. Totally fine."

"Still?" he asks. "We have an appointment with Dr. Hanna in fifteen minutes."

"Shit." I completely forgot. Chloe slipped me the card for an ob-gyn, and when Dante learned most women have their first appointment between eight and ten weeks, he insisted on making it for me. "Are we just fucked?"

"No, because I drove here when you didn't return to the apartment on time." Dante sighs. "We can make it if Armando drives."

I look at the notoriously insane driver sitting across from me. "Can you drive to the doctor?"

He nods. "That's what I was trying to warn you about. The appointment."

Damn it. My head's been fuzzy since the funeral.

"He'll do it." I hang up before Dante can reply and gather my things quickly. Before we leave, I walk up to Sal and hand him the chip. "Tony needs this before sundown. Tell him to put it in while the car's off, restart it, and do a basic set-up. He'll understand."

Sal nods. I gesture to Armando, and we rush off through the halls.

Dante sits at the curb, idling in a plain black sedan that I know has an engine to make drag racers weep under the hood. He thought he was going to have to chase me somewhere. When I meet his gaze, I see the fear painted there.

"Sorry." I slide into the backseat. "Tony—"

Dante waves my words away as he joins me in the back, leaving Armando to crack his knuckles before taking the wheel.

"I'm just happy you're okay." Dante kisses my knuckles. "I have a surprise for you later."

I nod. I'm already worrying about the midterms I'm going to have to work on when I get home. Hopefully, the surprise won't take too long.

Armando screams through the New York City streets. He grew up here, so he knows every road like the back of his hand, but he spent a decade in Italy after high school, so he still drives like he's on one of those tiny little vespas. I've never met a man with a better sense of where his car ends, the exact moment at which he has to slam the brakes. I've also never ridden with him without a few new bruises and the overwhelming urge to dry-heave. Still, we pull up in front of Dr. Hanna's office with three minutes to spare.

"Thanks," Dante says weakly.

Armando shoots us a thumbs-up. "I'll park and wait."

I rub my elbow and climb out of the car, my head still ringing with blaring horns. The office is light and airy, and a pleasant-faced assistant ushers us back into a room quickly.

"Okay, we've got a gown for Mommy." She places a folded piece of fabric on the table next to me. "Take off everything–or everything below the waist. Dr. Hanna will be along shortly. Anything for Daddy?"

"Uh." Dante seems as caught off guard as I am by the titles. "No, thanks."

She nods with another brilliant smile, then bounces out the door. I stare at the gown.

"Need help, Mommy?" Dante asks.

I grimace. "Not if you're going to call me that."

He laughs. "Come on, I think it's cute."

"No way." I shake my head. "'Mommy' always sounded gross to me. I'll be Mama when the time comes."

When. Somehow, that sounds weird. I begin stripping off my sweatpants.

"Mama." Dante wanders away to futz with a model of a uterus. "I can get on board with that. Would I be Baba?"

Abruptly, the scent-memory of Baba's blood on the carpet turns my stomach. I shake my head. "Whatever you want. Not that."

"Okay." Dante rushes back to my side and takes my hand like I'm not naked from the waist down in the middle of a doctor's office. "I can be Dad, or Dada, or anything else."

I force a smile. Somehow, parental titles make even less sense attached to him. Someone knocks on the door.

"One second!" I scramble onto the table and place the gown on my lap. "Okay."

A woman in a white coat opens the door with a much less toothpaste-commercial-y smile. "Hi, I'm Dr. Hanna. You're Eleni?"

I nod. "And this is Dante. He's my fiancé."

"Wonderful." She steps in and closes the door. "Since we've got a lot to go through today, I don't want to take too much of your time, but I like to tell new patients a little about myself. For one, I'm going to be with you from this first ultrasound to your due date. I think being able to trust your ob-gyn is the most important thing during a pregnancy. And with that"—she sits in a chair in front of me—"I also believe what you think is the most important. A doctor is a lot of different things to different people, especially for something as complicated as this. So, do you want me to be a friend? A comfort? A professional? You come first in here, Eleni."

That actually knocks me for a loop. I just kind of assumed she'd be...whatever she was going to be. The woman who sticks needles and wands into me to check on the baby. Dante takes my hand and squeezes it.

"Um," I say. "How about you do… maternal?"

She grins. "Awesome."

2 4

FOR REAL

"OKAY, this might feel a little strange. Just take a deep breath." Dr. Hanna inserts the ultrasound wand, the very last step of the appointment.

I breathe through the weirdness, and a grainy, black-and-white picture pops up on the screen. In the middle of a big patch of darkness sits a little grain of white.

"There's your baby," she says quietly. "It's too early to tell sex, but do you see right there?" She points to another bump on the screen.

I lean closer. Dante holds onto my hand like a lifeboat in a storm. "Yeah?"

"That's an eye." She smiles at me. "You're right on track, nine weeks pregnant."

I nod. The picture on the screen is...strange. It doesn't look like a baby yet. It looks like the thing they show pregnant women on TV that makes them cry.

Dr. Hanna looks at me for a moment. "Let me guess. You haven't started showing yet, and you're young, so you're having trouble believing you're really going to give birth."

I bite my lip. "You could do the maternal a little less well."

She laughs. "That little baby in there has a heartbeat. Would you like to hear it?"

I don't look at Dante. I haven't since the appointment began. I can't. But his fingers clench around mine, certain proof he wants this. I nod.

Dr. Hanna flips a switch on the monitor, and a whooshing, underwater noise fills the room. The longer I listen to it, the more I can pick out the fluttery *ba-BUMP, ba-BUMP, ba-BUMP* beneath.

A heartbeat. My baby's heartbeat. The little boy or girl growing in my stomach, the son or daughter I'm going to raise to be better than I ever dreamed I could be. I blink, and tears streak down my face.

"Why is it so fast?" I whisper. "Is it okay?"

"Yes." Dr. Hanna smiles. "Right now, their heart should be beating about 160 times per minute, and this sounds perfect. It'll even out as they grow."

In my mind's eye, a girl with Dante's eyes sprouts from a toddler to a teenager in seconds. A boy with Baba's chin. A million children, all full of pieces of the people I've loved, grow in fast motion.

"Would you like the DVD?" Dr. Hanna asks.

I'm beyond words. I look up at Dante and find him crying silent tears above me, his gaze locked on the screen. He nods like he can't make the words come out either.

"All right." Dr. Hanna pats my shoulder. "I'll go get that set up, and then we're done for the day." She withdraws the ultrasound wand and leaves.

The noise of my baby's heartbeat echoes off the walls. Dante and I sit silently for a moment, both crying.

"I love them so much," I mumble.

"There is nothing I wouldn't do for our child," Dante replies.

The truth of that rings through my bones. I sit up. I'm ready to go home and play that on a loop until the day the baby is born. Sometime in May, Dr. Hanna said.

"Wait." Dante puts a hand on my shoulder. "I need to—while we can still—" He pulls out a small, velvet box and opens it to reveal a perfect replica of the engagement ring he gave me before my kidnapping.

My tears flow harder as I pluck it from the cushion and slide it back onto my finger.

"It's not the same." He turns my hand over and points to one stone on the back, a dark one I don't remember. "That's for Baby. I keep dreaming of them having my eyes."

I throw my arms around Dante's neck and cling to him like the world might tear me away. This is real. The man who loves me. Our child together. I can't forget that again. I pull back and look in his eyes.

"Send Armando home," I say. "And get a hotel. I'm not waiting."

Dante grins. "Only if you give me my ring back first."

Minutes later, Dante and I stumble into an Airbnb that turned out to be the only place nearby willing to give us a room. I cling to his neck, kissing every inch of skin I can reach. He half drags me over the threshold, grabbing handfuls of my ass.

"No games," I gasp between kisses. "No pretend. Just us. For real."

He claims my lips. "Nothing would make me happier."

I grind up into Dante, delirious with want. I need to prove all of this is real, once and for all. I need every inch of him with nothing in between. So the clothes are going to have to go.

He's barely kicked the door closed when I start tearing at his shirt. His jacket floats to the floor easily, and I can untie his ties blindfolded —literally—but the shirt buttons give me trouble. My hands shake to the beat of the tiny second heart within me. Dante starts to take over, then quickly grows impatient. With a grunt, he yanks on each side of the shirt. Buttons scatter to the floor. I laugh.

"We have to go home after this."

Dante grins sheepishly. "We'll leave your bra here and call it even."

My mouth falls open. "You wouldn't."

He waggles his eyebrows, then dives for my mouth once more. My knees weaken, and I nearly slump in his grasp.

"Not good for baby." He picks me up, bridal-style, and kicks open what looks most like the bedroom.

A tiny office/yoga studio stares back at us.

"I hate New York sometimes," Dante growls.

I laugh. "Try again, Daddy."

He wrinkles his nose. "Only if you never call me that again."

I seal the deal with a kiss. The next door is a bathroom with a drop-down tub, but the third is, finally, a bedroom. With a twin bed. Dante just stands there for a moment, dismayed.

"This is perfect," I murmur.

"What?" he demands. "I can barely fit on that thing."

I smile up at him, tears threatening again. My chest squeezes. "It's perfect. Unforgettable, and totally, completely real."

His confusion melts. "I'll never understand you."

I show him my ring. "You've got a lifetime to figure it out."

"Thank god." He kisses me again, carries me into the minuscule bedroom, and lays me down on the bed like I'm made of glass.

I shed my sweatshirt, tank top, and—eyeing him—the bra underneath, then my sweatpants and underwear. Dante strips off the remainder of his suit without destroying any of it, much to my disappointment. I reach for him, and he obliges with a smile. He cages me with his arms, holding his body carefully above mine. Only his cock brushes against me. I press a kiss to the taut muscles of his arms and wrap my legs around his waist.

"I'm not breakable," I remind him.

"But—"

I shake my head. "Luca couldn't do it. Camila couldn't. You think you're going to be the one?"

Dante stares at me for a long moment, dark eyes full of something I can only describe as awe. "Of course not. But I want more for you than not breaking. I want to put you back together."

My eyes sting with more tears. "Come here, you ridiculous man."

Already knowing what I'm asking for, Dante sinks his cock into me. I moan softly. Finally, his chest touches mine. I lock my legs around his hips, wind my arms around his neck, not allowing a breath of space between us. There will be enough time for that when I start showing. Right now, I want all of him. He thrusts forward.

The bed squeaks loudly, and we both laugh.

"Perfect," I say.

Dante shakes his head, then slips a hand between us and circles my clit. I drag my mouth over his chest and shoulders. We rock back and forth, squeaking as little as possible and laughing every time we do. Dante's leg falls off the bed. I drag him back in with a hand on the back of his thigh. When our orgasms wash over us, they aren't the wild, explosive blackouts of pleasure we've shared before. My orgasm is quiet, soft. Real.

"I love you," I whisper against his sweaty shoulder.

"I love you too."

The bed squeaks.

"And I hate this Airbnb!"

2 5

FLIRTING WITH DEATH

Dante

A couple days after El's first ob-gyn appointment, I pull up in front of the same stupid diner Henry keeps insisting we meet at. He called me in the dead of the goddamn night, like I'm not busy, and insisted we meet. Finally, I was able to talk him around to doing this at the crack of fucking dawn, so at least I didn't have to leave my pregnant fiancée before she woke up. I can see him sitting at the same table as always, but I pull out my phone. Let him sweat.

A few notifications, nothing particularly exciting. I open the one from Tony and skim it, then smile. Third Russian hangout down, more bodies floating in the Hudson. I've been letting him mostly run that while I focus on getting regular operations up to snuff, and he's been crushing it. The other day, I even saw Wing smile. He's turning out to be much better at handling our "allies" than I thought he would be.

With a sigh, I pocket my phone and slide out of the car. We might be locked in mutually-assured destruction, but I'd rather not get destroyed because I woke up too early.

117

Inside, it could be midnight or noon, as always. The same smattering of random customers and tired waitresses stud the place, and the reek of decades of fried foods stuffs my nostrils. I join Henry in the booth.

A waitress appears before I can even open my mouth. "Coffee?"

I nod. She produces a cup that's clean but so deeply coffee-stained after years of use it looks like it's already full, then pours me a cup to match the one already sitting in front of Henry. He hasn't gotten any better at disguises, either. Today, I've gone with 'exhausted middle-class runner': T-shirt with old sweat stains at the neck, swishy plastic pants, worn running shoes. I even added one of those stupid armbands for phones. With any luck, he'll realize I'm making fun of him and snap.

"What?" I ask when the waitress moves off.

"Don't take that fucking attitude, Dante," Henry hisses. "What the fuck are you doing?"

I smile and sip my coffee. Black enough to actually start to wake me up. "Don't know what you're talking about. Where's Jace?"

"Fuck off," he says. "You know good and goddamn well what I'm talking about."

"Camila?" I ask quietly.

"The whole goddamn mess!" He gestures broadly enough I worry he's going to hit his cup. "You wanna fucking know where Jace is? Rikers?"

I choke on my next sip of coffee. "What the fuck? You have to know that wasn't me."

"I know, I know." Henry shakes his head. "He stuck his dick somewhere it really didn't belong. But my SSA knows I was working with him, so now they're looking at me and the Russian boss I promised to take off the streets."

I thump my chest a few times, then wipe my mouth. Jace, arrested. That's only good news for me. Even for a dirty fed, he was a loose fucking cannon. But being looked at closer is the last thing I need.

"So, what?" I ask. "You want me to un-kill Camila? That's beyond even my powers."

Henry ignores my joke. "I want you to stop dropping bodies. I don't have authorization for these raids, so I can't claim they're mine, and before long, someone's gonna fucking ask who's doing them."

"Say it's infighting," I answer flippantly. "Russian-on-Russian violence."

Henry surges up from his seat and fists his hand in the neck of my T-shirt. He's fast, but he's not strong enough to drag me out of my seat like he obviously wants to. The gun he did a crap job hiding glints under his suit jacket. I keep a smile on my face.

"I don't know where you got the idea you're in charge here," I say quietly. "But I've got a good grip on your balls, and I'm happy to twist. Now let go of my shirt and sit before you find out what your name looks like on the morning news."

"You're not the only one with leverage, Cattaneo." He doesn't release me.

"Let me put it this way." I smile a little wider. "I know what they do to cops in prison. And I know how many friends I've got inside. So I'm happy to share a cell with you if you're stupid enough to put hands on me again, *capiche?*"

Henry lets go of my shirt and drops back into his seat. A few drops of coffee slosh over the side of his cup. "You're flirting with death. I'm not the only person who could take you down."

The accusation sticks tighter than it would have before El, before the heartbeat in that little office, but I sip my coffee like his words don't mean a thing to me. The waitresses don't seem to give a fuck about our little scuffle, at least.

"Do you have anything other than threats?" I ask.

Henry sighs. "Fyodor's not a totally uncommon name, but I did some digging, and I was able to connect it to a guy called Raskolnikov, who dropped off the map in Russia about a month before Fyodor started moving over here."

"Raskolnikov?" I blink a few times. "It's a fucking *Crime and Punishment* reference?"

Henry shrugs. "The last thing we needed was a psychopath with an education."

I stare into my coffee, trying to put the pieces together. They won't click. "Is that all?"

"Here's Raskolnikov's record." Henry slides a file clearly labeled "Interpol" across the table to me. "Basically the same shit. He hits hard and fast, leaves little trace. Nasty sonofabitch."

I flip through a couple pages. A nasty sonofabitch who's been in business for damn near three decades, if Henry's right about the connection. Someone like that isn't going to topple after a few lost warehouses. He knows how to pick up the pieces.

"I wish I had an undercover." Henry thumps his fist on the table, spilling more coffee. "They all got pulled after we rescued Eleni. Burnt."

I stare at the file. A guy like this needs to be taken down from the inside. Henry, for all his stupidity and tactlessness, is right.

"Anything else?" I ask.

"What?" Henry frowns.

"You drag me out of bed at the ass crack of dawn to yell at me and give me another name that leads nowhere." I gesture to the file. "Do you have something actionable, or can I go back to sleep?"

He shakes his head disbelievingly. "Sleep if you want to, Cattaneo. I'll be awake 'til this is done."

I shoot the rest of my coffee, wincing at the burn, and toss a couple of bucks on the table before walking out. The Saints need an inside man. Someone Camila never met, someone none of the Russians would've crossed paths with.

Only one name comes to mind.

2 6

COMMOTION

Eleni

That weekend, I lean my head back against the chair at the head of the circle and try to pretend like I'm listening to what Wife #12 has to say. I know her name. I know I know it. But Nicky insisted on brunch for this meeting, and the omelet Val has balanced on her lap is really testing the boundaries of my control over my stomach. I suck in a slow breath through my mouth, then exhale through my nose as one of the many, many parenting and pregnancy books Dr. Hanna suggested told me to. It doesn't help.

"…and that's why I think you should have the wedding here," she finishes.

"In the backyard?" Nicky asks incredulously. "Like they're hippies?"

Wife #12 pouts. "If you'd *listened*, you'd know I considered that and have several suggestions that would allow Eleni to be…close to home without seeming like someone who lives in a van."

I roll my eyes at Gianna. The wives have been itching to start planning my wedding, and a couple days ago, Nicky ambushed me

121

with an already half-planned meeting to do exactly that. I just agreed. My morning sickness keeps getting worse, and Wife #12's backyard plan is the best pitch I've heard yet.

"That's not good enough for our Eleni." Nicky glances at me. "Even if she's a little under the weather right now. No, St. Anthony's is…."

Her words fade out as another wave of nausea rocks me. I clamp down on it. Part of me doesn't know why I'm bothering anymore. It's beyond obvious that everyone here knows something is up. I'm not showing yet, thankfully, but they keep shooting me worried looks and leaving awkward pauses in the conversation, like they're waiting for me to confess. But ever since the appointment, it's been impossible to forget just how much my baby's life counts on me. I have to take care of them, and that means protecting them from gossip vultures like Nicky.

"A three-tier cake? No, with two hundred guests, we're going to need at least five," Nicky says.

I don't honestly think I know two hundred people, at least by name. In my mind's eye, I picture my wedding like the barbecue. Everyone squashed into clothes they wouldn't normally wear, awkwardly pretending we don't want each other dead. At the rate Nicky's going, I wouldn't be surprised to see Fyodor's name on the guest list. Gianna rolls her eyes dramatically at me, and I swallow a laugh. I don't give a fuck about the wedding anymore. I'm tired and sore. I'll put on whatever dress they pick out, walk whatever aisle makes them happy, as long as I get a piece of cake and some really spectacular sex with my husband when I'm done.

"Does anyone need more to drink?" Chloe asks. "I was going to get a refill."

All eyes in the room turn to me, waiting to see if I'll ask for the famously boozy lemonade. So far, I've been coasting on not drinking anything at all, so I shake my head again. Chloe takes other orders while I daydream about fucking Dante in the middle of the church, having him declare me his in front of the first two hundred people Nicky came up with.

A door slams. Voices filter into the sitting room from the foyer. I sit up and realize Chloe's already gone. When I glance at Gianna, a spark of mischief shines in her eyes. What the hell is happening now?

"Eleni Calimeris," a very familiar voice demands. "Are you really going to leave your mama standing in the hallway? After not calling for weeks?"

Time turns to molasses around me. My heartbeat roars in my ears. I stand, holding onto the chair, half certain I'm going to faint if I let go. I'm not imagining things. Mama stands in the entrance to the sitting room, outlined in golden midmorning light. Gianna leaps up and sprints to my side, supporting me as I wobble the few feet over to Mama and throw my arms around her.

Mama hugs me back like a miracle, then stiffens.

"Keep going," Gianna says. "We can present ideas to Eleni once she's done receiving company."

Nicky immediately launches into a tirade about how a certain type of crystal is over-used.

Mama whispers in my ear, "When were you going to tell me you were pregnant, *zouzouni?*"

I pale. Suddenly, the extra few feet of distance from Val's omelet might not be enough to keep me from getting sick.

Gianna rubs my shoulder. "Take her into the kitchen."

I don't know which of us she's talking to, but Mama releases me from her hug and lets me lean on her as we stumble into the pale kitchen. Thankfully, all of the egg remnants were destroyed in here, and the air smells clean. Mama deposits me on one of the stools and crosses her arms.

"Did I raise you to be stupid?" she asks.

I shake my head.

"Reckless?" She raises an eyebrow.

I shake my head again. "Mama—"

"Then what on Earth made you try to do this with me?" she demands. "*Zouzouni,* this is what mothers are for."

Tears pressed against the backs of my eyes. "I know, Mama. I'm sorry."

She hugs me again briefly, then steps back again and takes my chin in one hand, tilting my face this way and that.

"You haven't been eating enough." She tuts. "Don't lie to me, I know it. I can see it in your face."

"I haven't been hungry." I rub my stomach. "Or baby hasn't."

Mama spits three times over my shoulder, more noise than action. "Don't mention the baby without that. They must be born safe."

That does coax a smile to my face. I remember Mama doing that for all our neighbors when I was growing up, and when Theia Adriani was having her children. It feels like becoming part of something.

"You're nauseous, yes?" she says.

I nod. "Every day, way outside the morning."

She studies me. "How far along are you?"

"Nine weeks." I look at the ground. "Sorry, Mama."

She shakes her head. "You should be. But nine weeks...hm, a month of sickness left." She turns to the refrigerator and opens it. "What is your Dante thinking? This food is no good." She pushes containers around for a few moments, then emerges with her arms full. "In the morning, you have Greek yogurt"—Mama sets the tub down with a thump—"with lemon, if you can handle it"—another thump—"and some cut-up fruit." She smacks an apple down next to the other two things. "This is fine, but peaches were better for me. Did your doctor give you vitamins?" She freezes and stares at me. "Did you go to the doctor yet?"

Dante enters the room with a laugh. "Not only have we been to the doctor, we have an ultrasound to show you. Baby has a heartbeat already."

Mama starts to tear up, but she makes the spitting noise again quickly. Dante raises an eyebrow at me. I shrug.

"If you think one video will make me forget you forced my *zouzouni* into a shotgun wedding, you're wrong." She sniffles. "But I would very much like to see my grandchild."

Dante circles around to put a hand on my shoulder. "I am sorry about that, Mama. The timing obviously isn't ideal."

"Isn't ideal." She scoffs. "Is that why you have no food? Have you been making sure she sleeps? Or have you been hogging the whole bed like nothing has changed?"

He grins. "Eleni's the bed hog, of the two of us, and I've been putting her to sleep as early as I can pull her away from her books."

Mama shakes a finger at him. "Pull harder. She is asleep by nine, no negotiation. My *zouzouni* won't listen to me, so you must."

"I'm right here!" I protest, but I can't imagine anything better than being pinned between the two people I love most in the world while they argue over how to take care of me.

The three people. Baby can't talk yet, but I love them as much as Dante and Mama already. In my mind, I make the spitting sound. A silly old tradition maybe, but I'd rather be safe.

"But will you listen?" Mama doesn't wait for an answer. "Of course not. So I must go around you."

I laugh and look at Dante over my shoulder. Once again, he brought Mama here without asking me. Part of me wants to be upset. She is my mother to tell, after all. But I needed her, especially now, and Dante could tell. It's hard not to love him for that.

I grin. "How long are you staying, Mama?"

"Now that I've seen you?" She lifts my chin again. "You would be lucky to get me out of here before the baptism."

27

RUBBING ELBOWS

Dante

Monday morning after Mama arrives, I move her into the apartment in the city with El and Gianna.

"Are you certain you can carry this?" She furrows her brow at the three suitcases in my hands.

I nod, trying to turn a grimace into a pained smile. I'm so happy she's here. I'm so happy El's happy. She has so much goddamn stuff.

With another frown, she waves me ahead of her, and I stumble into the lobby of the building.

Tuesday afternoon, I tap my foot on the floor of the elevator. I managed to sneak out between meetings just in time to meet Eleni when she comes home from classes and steal a few minutes. Usually, my Tuesdays are jam-packed, so I'm hoping to surprise her. I fidget with the bouquet of flowers I picked up on a whim.

Ding. The elevator doors open, and the first sound that greets my ears is high, feminine laughter. I frown. I checked her schedule. El shouldn't be back yet.

"Hello?" I call.

The laughter cuts off.

"We're in here!" Gianna yells from what sounds like the living room. If I'm not misreading things, she also sounds a little guilty.

I rush through the apartment and find her and Mama on one of the couches, surrounded by old pictures. I peer closer. Old pictures of Gianna and I's shared childhood.

"Your baby will be beautiful." Mama holds up one of me in the bathtub at about two, grinning and visibly naked.

"Why are these out?" I ask, holding onto shreds of my calm.

The elevator dings again, and my stomach drops. That's El. Gianna calls her in immediately, and she disappears into the pile of pictures. Her smile warms my heart, but I have to leave before I can do more than kiss her on the forehead. The flowers end up in a vase decorated with my baby pictures by the time I get home again.

WEDNESDAY, I set Gianna up with a late interview with a friend of mine who owns a club. She's been dancing on a circuit since Piacere burnt down in between classes, but I know she's looking for something more stable. Eleni arranges a call between Mama and her sister late enough that it's morning in Greece. When I step off the elevator with a bag of fragrant takeout from several different locations, Eleni is there with a tired smile on her face. I lean in for a kiss.

She cups my cheek. "I love you, but I'm starving. Food first?"

I agree with a laugh. We settle at the dining room table, and she lights a candle. The food spreads out like a banquet before us, and we eat, laugh, talk. I hold her hand for what feels like the first time in ages. Classes are going well. Her morning sickness is going strong. She combines stir fry and chicken parm in a nauseating combination that makes her sigh with happiness. I lean in to kiss her, and—

"*Zouzouni!*" Mama calls.

I wince back. El smiles apologetically.

"Theia Adriani has some advice on the first trimester." Mama barges into the dining room, pulls up a chair, and sits between us.

I take Thursday off, by some miracle. Thursday morning, Gianna can't work the blender. Thursday afternoon, she and Mama insist Eleni needs to go shopping for maternity clothes right then. Thursday evening, Eleni has homework, Gianna has a date emergency, and Mama needs to talk to me about "my plans." Thursday night, El and I fall into bed next to each other, exhausted.

Friday afternoon, I have business setting up the undercover agent Henry so unwittingly suggested, and I'm tired of leaving things to chance. I schedule my meeting for later than I usually would and park my car in front of Tandon to wait for her. Right on time, she emerges from the building with Armando next to her and the other two guards a safe distance away. When she spots me leaning against the car, her face lights up, and she charges the remaining distance for a hug. I wrap my arms around her and inhale her scent.

"This is going to really complicate the rumors that I'm dating Armando." She laughs and presses kisses to my mouth. "What are you doing here?"

I grin. "I thought you might need to get out of the apartment."

Her smile widens. "You're a genius. Where are we going? I'm not exactly wearing date clothes."

I look at the T-shirt and jeans she's started wearing to class, a compromise between her preference and her classmates' sweatpants. "I brought a change of clothes, don't worry. And while I'd love to take you out, I am very busy after Thursday."

She laughs ruefully. "What, that wasn't your perfect day off?"

I glance at Armando over her shoulder and lean in to whisper in her ears, "You know damn well my perfect day off involves you never leaving my bed."

El shivers, and I nip her earlobe behind the curtain of her hair. Fuck, I wish I could take her home and ruin her. Take her anywhere. But I really can't skip this.

"No, I thought you might want to do a little work with me. You are queen of the Saints, aren't you?"

She grins. I open the door to the town car I drove over here, hoping for at least a moment of quiet in the back. Armando takes the driver's seat without a word.

On the drive, I help her change into the leather pants, camisole, and blazer she wears for business, dragging kisses over exposed slivers of her skin. Between the darkened windows and the privacy divider, it feels like we're alone for the first time since Mama arrived. The button on her pants barely fastens, and I focus my attention on the slowly rounding bump of her belly, the heartbeat of our child echoing in my ears.

Armando pulls to a stop, and I open the door to show her the dingy alley that leads to Benny's, the ex-Coppola headquarters in the city. Eleni looks at me questioningly.

"I had an interesting conversation with my least-favorite friend the other day." This has become our euphemism for Henry. I know most of the men assume it means Cal. "And he mentioned the usefulness of eyes behind the Iron Curtain."

Eleni lets me help her out with a nod. "I thought your least-favorite friend already had those. What about Yagdash?"

"He went blind." We walk down the alley arm-in-arm. Armando stays in the car. "And anyway, those were his eyes. We're here to set up our own."

Eleni smiles. "Let me guess, my job is the trail."

"I knew you got into Tandon for a reason."

She snorts, and I open the door to allow her into the dingy dive. A new bartender mans the front, and the place is dead. Teo alone sits at the bar.

El frowns. "Teo? He's your undercover?"

"Hey!" He stands as he spots us. "Long time, no see!" He opens his arms for a hug.

Eleni, ever careful, hugs him with her pelvis angled away so he couldn't possibly feel the bump, then kisses him on both cheeks. I shake his hand, and all three of us sit.

"I didn't know I'd be meeting the whole royal family." Teo grins. "So are we a go?"

El still looks worried. I nod.

"Teo was my first choice. Only choice, really. He's not well-established with any organization, but he's been around the life for ages. And he has the look," I say.

Teo turns his face this way and that, showing off his fair hair and high cheekbones. "I even have a Russian great-grandmother, Lenora Valentinovna. I've been building up my collection of tattoos and putting out feelers, but they're starting to look into me, to see if I'm legit."

"That's where you come in," I say to her. "We need to set up a trail for him, Veniamin Valentinovich, from here."

Eleni looks from me to Teo and back again. "That's not enough. Do you have any idea how dangerous what you're talking about is? Do you know what they do to snitches?"

Teo nods. "Pretty much what they do to snitches everywhere else. And it'll be a lot more dangerous if you don't help. I'm tired of seeing the sons of bitches run my city."

She sucks her lip between her teeth. "What's your goal?"

"Just find Fyodor's home location," he answers. "Come on, it's no more dangerous than marrying the boss."

Eleni smiles slowly. "I guess we all take risks in war."

She launches into a list of details she needs to make this foolproof, and I smile. God, she's hot like this.

2 8

GOOD TO BE QUEEN

ELENI

IN THE CAR on the way back to the apartment, I'm practically vibrating. I hadn't even realized how much hanging around with Mama and Gianna, constantly being worried over and interrupted, was affecting me. Leave it to Dante to see what I can't and give me a chance to feel powerful again. I run my hand over his thigh.

"I don't suppose you got rid of the two of them?" I ask.

He smirks. "Why? Do you want something?"

"I might." I smile. "But I asked you first."

Dante meets my gaze, his dark eyes burning. "I absolutely did not."

I throw my head back against the seat. "Fuck!"

He laughs, very meanly, I might say. For the rest of the car ride, I pout. I'm an adult with a fiancé who has more money than anyone I've ever met. I should be able to have sex whenever I want. Dante takes this grumbling with a teasing smile, like it's all the funnier for him how much I want it. Asshole.

Armando pulls the car into the parking lot, and we get out. My phone vibrates. A text from Gianna.

Your mom had an idea for dinner, but we don't have the ingredients. Neither does anywhere nearby. We're headed to Little Greece, return ETA like, an hour.

A few kiss emojis finish the message, and I grin before tucking it into my pocket. Dante doesn't need to know. Yet.

We climb into an elevator, just the two of us, and he hits the button for our floor. As soon as the elevator starts moving, I throw myself at him. My lips meet his like a thunderclap, and despite all his teasing, his hands are on me before his brain seems to catch up.

"They might be waiting for us," he hisses against my mouth.

"Fuck 'em," I say with all the confidence of someone who knows we have nothing to fear. In an hour, I'll be a pregnant twenty-three-year-old with homework to finish again. Right now, I just want to be Queen of the Saints, powerful and sexy. I cup Dante's cock through his pants.

He reacts almost instantly, stiffening with a groan. I drag my teeth over his lips and palm him rhythmically.

"'S not a private elevator," he manages.

"Good." I grab one of his hands and shove it up under my shirt. I'm still just wearing the casual T-shirt bra I picked for school, but he responds like it's my laciest lingerie. He's already so hard.

"Do you touch yourself on Staten Island, thinking of me?" I whisper.

"I'd rather touch you." He fits his hand inside my bra and plucks at my nipple. I arch against him.

The elevator dings. I pray it's our floor and spin away.

A haggard-looking businessman steps on. He glances at us briefly, turns red, and whips his gaze away before hitting his button, a few floors up. My heart pounds. This complete stranger nearly caught us. After all this time being worried about, coddled, fussed over, that is electric. I set myself up for this and Dante let me. I slide my hand over the front of his pants to his still achingly hard cock, and he inhales sharply through his nose. He meets my gaze, a silent request for my color. I mouth, "Green," and squeeze him. He drops his head back against the wall of the elevator.

Three floors. That's how long I play with Dante through his pants while he tries not to make a noise. The wash of control is intoxicating. I'm not just a fragile baby factory. I am Eleni Calimeris, a name known and feared in New York City.

The elevator stops again, and the businessman leaves.

"Finish what you started." Dante's voice is hoarse. "Use your mouth."

That is an easy command to follow. I drop to my knees on the floor of the elevator and open his pants. His cock springs free, the head shining, and I barely take a breath before Dante threads his hands into my hair and forces me onto it.

"You little slut," he mutters. "Couldn't wait. Needed me so goddamn bad. Making a mess of me like I don't know just how to make a mess of you."

I moan around his shaft, and he thrusts his hips forward sharply. Tears prick at the corners of my eyes. I grin. He can say what he wants, but he's the one falling apart. His taste is rich on my tongue already.

The elevator *dings* again, and this time, there's no hiding. Part of me hopes it's our floor. The rest doesn't matter.

"Gianna?" Dante calls. "Maria?"

I don't stop moving. I know what silence will answer him.

"They're gone." He groans. "Out of the elevator and take your shirt off."

I release him, a thin string of saliva connecting his cock to my mouth, and scramble backward on my knees. Once I'm properly in the apartment, I begin shedding clothes. Jacket, camisole, bra. Dante watches me for a long moment, then steps forward. I open my mouth to accept him once more.

He grabs my hair and yanks me back. "No, you don't deserve that." He takes his cock in hand, jerks it a few times, and hot strings of come splatter on my face and chest.

I lap up the little that lands in my mouth with a smile. "We have an hour."

Confusion mars Dante's face, followed by realization, followed by a thrillingly dangerous darkness. "You knew they weren't here."

I nod.

"You hid that from me."

I lift my breasts to my mouth and begin cleaning them. "Aren't I the queen?"

Dante takes a step closer. "A queen listens to her king."

I look up at him, my tongue coated in his taste. "Make me."

Something sparks in his gaze, and he yanks me up off the floor, then grabs one of my sticky nipples. I expect him to toy with me, but he drags me to the bedroom by that slim, sensitive flesh. I whimper and stumble after him. When we reach the bedroom, he throws me down onto the bed and turns away.

"Strip." He shuts the door. "I won't be interrupted by their impromptu arrival."

I shimmy out of my pants and underwear, that rush of control still sparkling in my veins. I made him do this. There is control in obedience, in submission too.

"Hands and knees." A familiar drawer rattles. Our toys. I assume the position.

The first smack of the riding crop lands hot against my ass without warning. I rock forward, yelping.

"Count," he growls. "When you reach ten—correctly—I'll stop."

"One." My voice rings out, strong and certain.

By four, this is no longer true. More tears bead in my eyes. Dante is an expert at hitting the same spot over and over again, pushing the relatively easy to handle pain of the riding crop as high as the paddles and belts he says he won't use on me until I give birth.

The next hit lands somewhere new. "Six!"

Dante tsks. "Five. Again."

By my counter, we're around twenty-five by the time I manage to mumble "ten" correctly. Tears sheet down my face. My ass burns. My whole body aches with want.

Dante swipes a finger between my legs, gathering the wetness there. "You really are a slut. You were this wet on the elevator, weren't you? When that man walked in?"

I nod, beyond words.

"You wanted me to bend you over and fuck you right there, huh?" His voice moves behind me.

I am beyond wondering what he's doing. I nod again.

He hums, palms the white-hot skin of my ass. "Poor little pet. But I don't share."

Just like my mouth, he grabs my hips and yanks me onto his cock. My arms give out, and I topple onto my elbows with something like a scream. I don't know how long it's been. I don't care. I just know I need him exactly where he is, pounding into me like he knows I can take anything he dishes out. I sob into the comforter.

"Come for me, pet," he murmurs. "Just me."

Pleasure explodes through me. Dante fucks me through it, into a second orgasm, a third, each so close on the heels of the last I barely know my own name by the time he pulls out and I slump, boneless, to the bed.

He kisses me softly on the shoulder. "We've got about fifteen minutes. How about I run you a bath, and when they get home, they won't be able to say anything until you're out?"

It's good to be the queen.

2 9

DREAMS

I ADJUST the zoom lens on the camera, and the street below snaps into focus. Four twenty-somethings stroll down the sidewalk in the summer sunset, talking loudly to each other. The lankiest one says something that makes the bleached-blonde leader punch him. The final two laugh. With another twist, I zoom in on the only one we care about. Teo—Veniamin, as these fucks know him—cocks a fist back to hit the lanky one again, but the leader shakes his head. Together, the four of them enter a crappy electronics shop we've learned is yet another Russian front. I sit back from the camera.

"How's it look?" Mikey asks.

Like Dante sent another kid just about Seb's age into the goddamn lion's den without thinking. The phantom Seb in my mind shakes his head. He talks less than he used to, since the funeral, but I can't fucking get him to go away.

"They look like besties." I shrug. "'Nother guy in the group got hit. Not Teo."

Mikey nods. The sunset makes him look even older than he is, highlighting all the fine lines in his face. Seems fucked up that he's really only got ten years on me.

"How much longer do you think it's gonna be?" I ask.

Fucking stupid. I'm leading this watch, this whole goddamn mission now that Dante set it in motion. I should have the answers, not be asking for them. Mikey, who's been a Saint since Dante's dad was new, looks at me like he knows that.

"I'm thinking a few more days. That's Artyom's place, and the other intelligence says he's the obschak, at least for this neighborhood," I say.

"Bookkeepers always matter." Mikey nods.

Silence falls. I ignore the phantom Seb dangling his feet off the edge of the rooftop. Fucking kid did that when he was alive, too. At least now I don't have to worry about him falling.

"Where's Dante tonight?" Mikey asks. "I would've thought he'd be here for something like this."

The implication is obvious. I bristle right the fuck up. "He's working the business. You really think the boss needs to waste his fucking time on a rooftop? That's what he's got morons like us for."

Mikey puts up his hands. "Hey, no offense intended. I just keep noticing he's not around when he would've been."

"And I keep noticing your wife looking lonely," I bite back. "Need me to pay a visit out to bumfuck nowhere, cheer her up?"

He scoffs and takes one of the folding chairs we've brought up here for the long night of watch. "Fuck me, I didn't intend to set off the attack dog. Just figured you might know more."

Seb furrows his eyebrows. He's curious. Goddammit, I am too.

"About what?" I take the seat next to Mikey. We'll hear when Teo leaves. His posse is loud as fuck, and he'll signal us if something goes wrong inside.

"I just mean…." Mikey shakes his head. "It's different for him now. Adri and I have been living this life for a while, but everyone adjusts at their own pace."

Because of Eleni. Everything circles back to fucking Eleni. I feel like a bastard every time I think it, but sometimes I wish she'd never caught Dante's eye. Then, I wouldn't be having endless fucking conversations with capos and "allies" about Dante quitting the life. I shove up from my chair and march across the rooftop to the cooler we hid in the sliver of shade before the sun started setting. Mikey drinks dad beer, so I grab him his light shit, and a bottle of craft porter Seb had in the back of the fridge for a special occasion. I know he would want me to drink it, even if it tastes like dirt. With the tip of my pocket knife, I pop both caps off and return to the seat.

"What adjustment do you need, out there in Jersey?" I ask. Dickhead question, but Mikey's being a dickhead, and he knows better than to take me personal.

"Every time I leave the house, I gotta wonder if tonight's the night I call Adri from the last burner phone hidden on my person, tell her to grab the cash out of the attic, take the kids, and disappear," he says bluntly. "Every goddamn time. You need balls of steel to survive that, and I'm not saying Dante doesn't, but…we don't know if he does, you know?"

Seb straightens, worried.

"We?" I ask. "You been talking to the other guys about this?"

Mikey shakes his head. "Not on purpose, anyway. The rest of the guys fucking love Eleni, and they know what the two of them have been through. There aren't any rumblings to worry about. People are just curious."

Mark me down for that. I feel like I spend half my goddamn nights now, wondering what's gonna happen next. Will we drop the Russians? Will the triads and Cal team up and drop us? What the hell happens when all of this breaks? Am I ever gonna stop seeing my little brother out of the corner of my goddamn eye?

"You know, I didn't think Dante was ever going to be boss," Mikey says.

"What?" I knew since the first day I met him.

"Did you see him in college?"

I nod.

"He had a career in football if he wanted it." Mikey stares at the horizon. "One in business too, proper business. He pulled grades like no kid I've ever seen in the life."

The grades, I fucking remember. Back then, I'd seriously considered throttling him so he'd stop coming home with a higher GPA to compare to my higher body count.

Mikey shrugs. "I just thought he'd get out is all."

I nod slowly. I never thought that. Not until recently, when he joined up with the goddamn feds to get her back. I barely feel like I know him anymore. Maybe he doesn't have the steel balls Mikey is talking about.

Fuck, I'm going to have to lead the Saints.

Seb hops up and does a silent victory dance.

30

THE OLD PLACE

Eleni

I LEAN BACK in my seat and groan. "Too...much...food..."

Gianna laughs. "Once you give birth, I'm getting you into pole. Even if you never perform, it burns calories like a mother—"

Mama starts to frown, and Gianna stops. I laugh. She's been working on her language.

"Well, it'll let you eat as much as you want," Gianna says quickly.

Mama nods. "If you don't perform, I think that would be all right with Dante."

Gianna launches into a list of how many dancers Dante has gone out with, seemingly just to scandalize Mama, and I look around the homey surroundings. To celebrate the end of my midterms, Mama suggested we go to Zorba's Tavern, a warm, blue-and-white-walled little restaurant back in the old neighborhood. We used to come here every time Christos or I got all As in school. I tried to explain I didn't have my grades back yet, but she was adamant. She couldn't celebrate my last grades, or me getting into Tandon, so we were going to Zorba's.

"Well," Mama says. "I suppose some…standards might be different here."

Gianna snickers. Mama's working on her language, and she's working on Mama's sex positivity.

Demi, the forty-something waitress who's been here since I was a kid, swans over to our table with the check. "You ladies all done, or do you want to eat us out of house and home?"

Mama laughs. "If you only had this much food back in Greece, you'd lose your house, home, and land before the weekend."

Demi smiles and sets the check down. "Thank goodness my mama moved, then. Are you back?"

"Just for a little." Mama's smile fades, but she takes my hand. "My Eleni is getting married."

Demi's mouth drops open. "Little Eleni? Show me the ring!"

I display my hand, and within minutes, a restaurant's worth of Greek women are fawning over me, asking questions about Dante, suggesting the best Orthodox churches for the ceremony. Gianna laughs at first, but she blends right in soon enough. My chest aches. If Frank Lombardi never got Baba under his thumb, my engagement would've been like this the whole time. But I wouldn't have Dante.

"Now, Maria, you have no excuse to stay away," an elderly woman whose name I've forgotten declares. "The Greek Corner is up for rent finally. You march down there and put your name in right now!"

Mama's face falls. "For rent?"

The mood dips.

"Didn't you hear?" asks Demi. "I assumed you were around to look."

Mama shakes her head. People say a few more encouraging things, then start to drift back to their own tables. Quiet falls over the restaurant.

"Baba always promised we'd buy that building, just as soon as we had the money," Mama whispers. "To see it rented to someone else…."

I put my hand over hers. I got my last goodbye to the Greek Corner, the day after we lost Baba. Mama never said goodbye. "Do you still have the keys?"

She looks up at me, shocked. "Eleni Calimeris, are you suggesting we break into a building?"

I shrug and smile. "It wouldn't be the worst thing I've done."

Mama pales. She doesn't ask about my work with the Saints, so I don't even know what she's imagining, but I know she wishes I wasn't involved.

Gianna stands. "I'm going to go get a cup of coffee. There's a place around here I'm obsessed with, and I'm happy to swear up and down you're going with me."

Mama looks from Gianna to me. That's not a "no" or a "what are you thinking?".

She takes a deep breath. "I will join you shortly."

I squeeze Mama's hand. "We will."

Gianna flounces out of the restaurant with a grin. I pay the check, and Mama and I cut through the back way to the Greek Corner. She holds her nose as we pass the dumpster between buildings, and the gesture is so familiar I almost want to cry. How many nights did we walk this way, did Christos tease Mama by drawing in lungful after lungful of stink?

We arrive at the back door of the building. Mama withdraws the key from her purse, the same old key with the half-broken clay gyro keychain I bought her one Christmas. She slots it into the knob and turns.

The door opens. Mama sucks in a sharp breath.

"This isn't smart," she says.

"No, it's not." I tighten my grip on her hand. "But Dante will take care of us if we get arrested."

Mama giggles, sounding young for the first time in a long time. With another deep breath, she steps inside. The air is deathly still, and for a split-second, the thick smell of copper coats the back of my throat. If we walk upstairs, the carpet will still be stained with Baba's blood. If we walk forward, the tables will still be knocked over and the register open.

The smell disappears into nothing more than bleach as Mama

makes a small sound. I turn and find her staring around the empty half-pantry that leads into the kitchen.

"It's like a mussel someone emptied," she says, her voice weak and wet.

Before I can answer, she releases my hand, unlocks the door to the back of the restaurant proper, and pushes it open. The bleach smell intensifies. Inside there's just…nothing. The shelves on the bodega half stand empty. No chairs or tables clutter the floor. No register on the counter. Even the light boxes above the counter where we put the see-through sheets of the menu are blank like staring eyes. Mama sinks to the floor.

"We bought it just like this, your baba and I," she says. "Back then, it looked like potential."

I sit next to her. I've never seen Mama like this, not even in the days after Baba's death. She's not quite sad. Just shellshocked.

"What did you imagine?" I ask.

She smiles at me. "You and that imagination. I always knew you were going to find your own path."

"Tell me, Mama." I put a hand on her knee. "I don't want to talk about me right now."

She laughs. "Fine, fine. Boss an old woman around." She shakes her head. "I imagined exactly what we ended up with. Shelves full of food, chairs and tables, regular customers. Your baba was the dreamer. He thought we'd be able to take out the shelves and become a full-service restaurant. Sit-down dinners." She drops her voice into an approximation of his. "Tourists from everywhere begging for your cooking, *astéri mou.*"

I can hear him perfectly. I swallow against a sudden lump in my throat.

"This is why Christos was never going to settle down like we wanted him to." She smiles as the first tear drops down her cheek. "He wanted to dream like your baba, but he didn't have the—the—*apofasistikótita.*"

"Determination," I fill in.

She nods. "He wanted his things easy because Baba made things easy." She sniffles. "I miss them both."

I've been crying easier since I got pregnant, but I don't even notice the tears falling until Mama wipes them away this time.

"Tell me, *zouzouni*," she says.

I open my mouth to promise I'm fine, and everything spills out instead. How distant I feel from my classmates. How scared I am about bringing a little life into such a scary world. How I think Dante might be getting tired of this life too, but I know I can't leave without him. The night Dante and I talked about moving to Greece with her—less a lot of the details.

Mama just nods and strokes my hair and lets me talk. Fuck, Chloe was right. I did need her.

"—so I don't know what to do," I finish lamely.

"Well," she says, "and do not take this as a mother's selfish whim, but your cousin Vlasis just graduated from NTU, in Athens, and he is a very important computer man now."

I laugh wetly. "I couldn't take that as anything. What's a computer man? What's NTU?"

She shakes her head. "You call yourself Greek. It is one of our best schools. He got a computer degree, and he works in a big tower. I didn't understand when he tried to explain."

What she's saying fits so neatly in with the life Dante and I imagined that I almost can't believe her. A university where I could actually, finally finish my degree in Greece. Safe and sound away from the violence of New York.

"What are you saying, Mama?" I ask quietly.

She kisses my forehead. "I am saying nothing at all, *zouzouni*. I love you, and you will dream your own path. My job is only to support you now."

I nod and stare at the papered-over windows of the restaurant that used to be ours.

BY THE BALLS

SOMETHING THUDS UPSTAIRS, and even though we know it's probably one of the other families in the building, Mama and I spook and scurry out. She nearly drops the keys as she locks the back door behind us, but by the time we emerge back onto the street, we're laughing.

"Is it really like this for you every day, *zouzouni?*" she asks breathlessly.

I gulp down air. Do I tell her about the nights I spend sitting awake, terrified? How often do I kiss Dante and think it might be the last time? How the heartbeat that made my baby real scares the absolute shit out of me because that's a whole, real person I'm responsible for?

"Yes and no," I say. "Should we find Gianna?"

Mama peers at me, then nods. She knows I'm hiding something. For her sake, all I care about is that she doesn't press.

NTU. Hm.

We find Gianna nursing three cups of coffee at a table outside the shop she mentioned. She waves as we approach.

"See? You were here the whole time." She gestures at the other two drinks.

Mama grimaces. "Coffee? At night?"

"Test it." Gianna smiles secretively.

Tentatively, Mama lifts the cup to her lips, then smiles. "How did you know I drink peppermint tea at night?"

"I smell it in the kitchen after I get home from work." Gianna laughs, then looks at me. "I got you decaf."

I groan and sip the bitter simulacrum of my favorite drink. "Thanks, I guess."

Mama shakes her head. "You'll be happy when baby comes out with the right number of limbs."

"I really don't think coffee does that," I say.

Mama makes the spitting sound and ignores me.

Gianna chuckles. "Shall we head back?"

"Fine." I glance around. Yep, there in the shadows stands Leo. I wonder whether he came with us or stayed with Gianna when we split up. I jerk my head in the direction of the apartment, and he nods. "Let's go."

As we walk, Mama and Gianna bicker about Mama paying her back for the drink. Gianna categorically refuses. Mama says she knows Gianna doesn't have steady work right now. And around, and around. It's sort of soothing, in its own way. They argue differently than Mama did with Christos, but it reminds me all the same.

My stomach kills. Not like I'm going to throw up—thankfully—but between the food baby resulting from dinner and baby, these pants really don't fit. Sneakily, I unfasten the button and drape my shirt over it. I'm not really showing enough for people to notice, but my jeans definitely have.

We turn a corner, and as is my habit now, I scan the street for anything out of place. Streams of busy New Yorkers pour this way and that, giving no sign dinner has come and gone. Tightly packed cars add to the choreographed chaos. My heartbeat synchs with the rhythm of the city. Hopefully baby's does too.

A sour note in the symphony catches my eye. Despite a blaring walk signal, a man stands against a streetlight, not moving. People shoot him dirty looks as they move past. Normally, I'd chalk it up to any of the million little incidents that knock the city out of harmony, but then he turns.

Henry Alcott. And he's making eye contact with me. Like he's waiting.

"Stay here," I say across Mama and Gianna's arguing. "You too, Leo."

Leo scowls. Mama and Gianna both try to follow where I was looking, but while Mama remains confused, Gianna's gaze narrows.

"No." She crosses her arms. "I'm going with you."

No one but me, Dante, and Tony know about Dante's arrangement.

"You're not." I cross my arms right back at her. "And if you try, I'll tell Dante you really want a bidet for your bathroom in the apartment."

Her mouth drops open. "You wouldn't."

Gianna hates bidets. "I very much would."

Before anybody else can argue—and as the walk signal starts to count down from ten—I turn and sprint across the street.

Ugh, maybe I am a little nauseous.

I arrive in front of Henry moments before cars begin screaming across the road again, and he looks down at me with a small smile.

"Ms. Calimeris," he says. "Or is it Cattaneo already?"

I tuck my engagement ring behind my back. "It's Eleni. What do you want?"

His smile grows. "I'm just on an evening constitutional. I was thinking this area would be such a nice place to live."

We're on the same block as the apartment. He knows where we live. And judging by the lumpy ankle of his suit, he decided to tell me he knows while armed.

"Really?" I summon up every last remaining thread of ice-Eleni. "I think it would be loud."

He shakes his head. "I grew up in the city. Quantico is the quietest place I've ever lived, and I graduated from the Academy some time ago now."

"You were in Chicago last, weren't you?" I smile prettily.

Henry's eyes flash. "I see why you and Dante work now. You both have a crap sense of when it's time to shut your mouth."

My temper blazes, and I take a step closer to him. The endless human tide of the city pays us no attention, and Henry can't be wired. Well, he can't be wired usefully. It's far too loud for usable audio.

"I know better than some turncoat fed snake," I hiss. "Tell me what the hell you want."

His irritation seems to burn brighter as I don't back down. "History has proven again and again that Dante can't protect you. Do you really want to try your luck with me?"

I look him up and down, from his greased-back hair to his poor imitation of Tony's good looks, and laugh. Every muscle in his body tenses at once.

"You think you have me by the balls, huh?" he snarls. "Well, let's fucking see who has whom. The Russians are making a mess right now, but who do you think is next on this list after them?" He smiles viciously. "Darling Dante and his Saints. I've got a RICO case that would make you *weep*, and I'm just waiting for a chance to pull the trigger."

Confidence lines his mouth, the clenching and unclenching of his fists. He'll do it. Fuck. I want to run away, curl up in a little ball, and figure out how to give birth to baby in a way that no one can tie them to me.

In my mind, I hear Mama's spitting noise. Warding off ill omens. Like Henry fucking Alcott, who I will not let see me flinch. Icy Eleni takes the reins, straightens my spine.

"Do it," I say. "But know that if you ever approach me again, if I see you waiting for me like this, *anything*, you're going to wish you never heard the name Calimeris."

"Good luck with that." He smiles, glances down. "By the way, your pants are unbuttoned."

My heart slams into my rib cage. The question "does he know" sets the pace of my frantic steps back across the street, my breathless explanation to Mama and Gianna. As we hurry away, I keep checking over my shoulder. Henry just remains against the streetlight, watching us.

Stepping into the elevator usually calms me. This place is damn near impossible to attack. Tonight, I just rub my belly, spitting mentally in threes. When we get inside, I tell Mama and Gianna I'm turning in for the night, head to the room, then grab my phone and dial Dante's number.

"El?" he says, confused.

"I want to sleep at the old place tonight." The words tumble out of my mouth. "We need to talk. Just us."

3 2

SNEAKY

Dante

"Quickly." I hang up the phone and sit back down at my desk. I don't know what the hell made El call me like that, but I know the driver headed her way needs to move fast. Anything that scares her, scares me.

Which means it's a bitch of a time trying to get my eyes to refocus on the work I was doing right before she called. I tap my fingers on the top of my desk, hum a song to myself, play music out loud. Nada. Finally, I give up, pour myself a glass of scotch, and take a long sip. Peaty. Rich. Steadying, thank God. When I sit back down at my desk, the words don't swim off my computer screen.

Windows crowd the monitor, all different transcripts of different reports from Teo since he's gone under. He said something when he came out this last time that scratched an itch in my brain, and I'm trying to figure out where that itch came from.

Klondike Paper. Apparently, it's the name of an office the Russians control, one they don't intend to let Teo into for a while yet. But I swear it sounds familiar. Another sip of scotch, and I turn to the next transcript.

If El were here, she could probably whip up a program to search the phrase in fifteen seconds flat.

But she's not, and I ran this goddamn syndicate before her. I shoot the rest of my drink and focus all my brainpower on the stupid screen.

Time ticks away.

And away.

And away.

Ah!

We stumbled in on a couple of, uh, brigadiers? Squad leaders. And they got quiet real fast when we showed up, but I heard the word Klondike. Like the ice cream or something. Anyway, I asked Vik who they were later, and he said they handled movement for Rodion.

That asshole needs to pick a less accessible reference. Immediately after Henry told me about his stupid Raskolnikov-Fyodor switch, I picked up a copy of *Crime and Punishment* and read the whole thing. Teo missed the main character's first name, but I'm not that stupid.

Klondike Paper. They have an office in the Bronx, and in that office, Fyodor might wait.

Or they know I'm working with Henry, who pulled the Interpol file, and they're using the *Crime and Punishment* reference to bait me.

"Fuck!" I shove back from my desk. Life would be so much easier if the Russians weren't so goddamn sneaky. This isn't the first lead we've gotten on Fyodor's location, just the one I've had to work hardest for, and they all disappear in a puff of smoke when we try to look into them.

With a sigh, I pull out my phone and dial Cal Duncan. What's the point of allying with a crazy Irishman if not pointing him at ghostly enemies?

He picks up quickly, and I wade through the pointless sea of his banter until he asks me what's going on.

"Got a location," I say. "Might be Fyodor."

I can almost hear him salivate over the phone. "Is that an invitation, boss man?"

"Better." I smile grimly. "It's an offer. Spot's all yours, if you want it."

He cackles. "So, you think it's shite."

"I'm not sure." The transcript stares blankly back at me. "If it's nothing, they're even smarter than I gave them credit for. Regardless, make it look like you just stumbled into the spot. We don't want them to know how close we are."

"Well, me and mine'll burn a Russian spot any time of night. I'll report with anything I find."

After that, we hang up quickly, and I have nothing to do but fidget until—

The door opens. Thank God, El's here. I jump out of my chair and race for the foyer. When I arrive, she stands in the middle of the room, her arms wrapped around herself and something burning in her beautiful blue eyes. She doesn't approach me, and worry prickles over my skin.

"Andre, Lucio?" she says.

The two guards flanking the door look at her.

"Go outside." Her voice is flat. "I'll let you know when to come back."

They obey wordlessly, and I know something is very fucking wrong.

"El, what—"

She puts up a hand to silence me. "Is there anyone else in here?"

I haven't hired a new chief of staff for the house since Andrea died, and I prefer my guards outside. I shake my head.

She slumps, and I rush forward to catch her. She lets me. Technically. But when she looks up at me, the emotion in her eyes resolves into tears and anger.

"What happened?" I ask.

"Henry fucking Alcott happened," she snaps. "Dante, he knows where the apartment is. He was waiting for me."

"That motherfucker." Anger bubbles under my skin. This is how he responds? Going after my fiancée? "Don't worry about him. I can end his career."

"I'm not worried about careers, I'm worried about lives." Eleni pulls out of my arms. "I'm starting to show, just a little, so I unbuttoned my pants on the walk home, and he noticed. What if he knows about baby? What difference does his fucking career make then?"

Just like her mother, she makes a spitting noise three times. I shake my head slowly.

"He doesn't," I say. "You're not showing enough. It could be anything. I have him under control, El, trust me."

"I trust you." Her tears leak into her voice, making it wobble. "It's him I don't trust. He's going to stab you in the back, and you're too cocky to see it."

"You don't know what I have." I smooth my hands over her shoulders. "Fuck, I'm sorry he got to you like that, but he's just swinging his dick around, trying to seem like more trouble than he is. I promise."

She sucks in a shuddering breath. "Are you sure, Dante? Sure enough to put baby's life on the line?"

For a second, I consider it. I'm not stupid. I have a suitcase of cash —several—stashed in this house. We could leave right now, go to ground, and let Henry have his stupid fucking pissing contest with someone else. But Cal and his boys might be ending the fight with Fyodor right now. And, if I'm being honest, I know Henry too well for him to scare me.

"I promise," I say.

She studies my face, looking for any hint that I don't believe myself. When she doesn't find it, a tentative smile blooms over her lips.

I lean in and kiss it.

33

BELIEF

Eleni

When Dante kisses me, for a split second, I think about pulling away. The fear and anger of my encounter with Henry still courses under my skin. There's so much to be scared about, enemies closing in from all angles.

Dante bites my lip, and endorphins flood my system. This is why I've stayed. He makes me feel like no one ever has. Not because he knows how to touch me, but because I can melt into his arms, let everything go, and trust he'll pick up the pieces afterward. I have nothing to fear with Dante.

And he promised. So I'll trust him.

I throw my arms around his neck. "I want to listen tonight."

He sweeps me off my feet in a bridal carry. I yelp.

"Shush," he reprimands. "Tonight, you hear me, pet."

I bite my own lip as he jogs up the stairs. The heavy mantle of submission steals over me, crushing the remaining fears from my system.

Dante veers into our bedroom and deposits me on the bed. "Do you particularly like these clothes?"

I look down at the blouse and jeans I wore to dinner. They can be replaced. "N—"

He raises an eyebrow. I flush, then shake my head.

"Good."

With a dangerous smile, he positions me. I grip the headboard with both my hands, and he has me stretch my legs as far apart and as wide as I can. Then, he begins undressing himself slowly, looking me over with appreciative eyes.

"Hold that," he says. "All of it. Eyes open. Mouth closed."

No restraints. No gags. I have no tools to rely on but the strength of my desire to obey. I meet his gaze and draw strength from his dark eyes. He believes I can do this. I won't disappoint him.

Gorgeously naked, Dante circles me like I'm prey. His muscles ripple under his olive skin. I shiver.

And he's on me. He attacks my mouth, my neck, the slim triangle of skin exposed by my modest blouse. A cry bubbles up inside me, and I force it down. I can't stumble at the first hurdle. I clench my fists around the headboard like it's his hair.

Dante unbuttons my blouse one by one, then continues his attack on each new inch of exposed skin. When he reaches the valley between my breasts, I nearly lose my composure. I have to look down at him to regain myself.

His dark eyes meet mine. A thin veneer of dominating control, near boredom as he waits for me to fail, lies over a pit of burning hunger. He wants me as much as I want him. Pleasure will come, if slowly.

The thin fabric of my blouse falls uselessly to the sides, exposing my bra. He lingers on my torso for long minutes, sucking dark bruises into my skin where no one will see them. The pain sparks, hot and bright, and I sink my teeth into my lower lip to stay quiet.

The sharp *snick* of a pocket knife flipping out breaks my focus. My attention whips from his face to the blade in his hand. Carefully, he threads it under the thin strip of the band that connects the two cups of my bra and yanks upward. The fabric splits instantly. Dante drops the knife and bares my breasts to his eyes. The warm puff of his breath coaxes another shiver from my body. He tuts, and I nearly break the command to keep my eyes open. He's so intense, so all-encompassing. I need the nothingness to get enough distance not to lose myself entirely.

With a scowl, he reminds me I asked to lose myself. When he laves a tongue over one of my quickly pebbling nipples, I stop fighting. I have nothing to fear. Dante will take care of me. My whole mind goes fuzzy as I submit to him entirely.

He spends ages on my breasts. Teasing, pinching, coaxing me to the edge of failure and pulling back just enough. He is a master with his instrument. He knows my body better than I do. All I have to do is lie back and turn into one quivering nerve, waiting for the next glance, the next touch.

Dante unzips my jeans and plunges one hand into them without preamble. It is nearly impossible not to curl around him, to yell his name. Tears burn my eyes. I stay still.

"So wet for me." He smiles indulgently. "I was worried. You were so quiet."

I shake my head, desperate for him to know what he's done to me. I'm just trying so hard to be good.

He laughs as he pulls his hand back out. "Do you think you can survive an orgasm without breaking?"

No, definitely not. I am about to nod, to beg, to lie about my capabilities out of need, but the haze of submission stops me. He wants me to be quiet and still. I want to listen.

My face burning, I shake my head again.

"You're so good." He cups my hot cheek. "I already knew that, but I would've let you prove yourself wrong. Since you were good though, pet, I'll make you a deal." He smiles. "I'm going to get the big vibrator."

My lower lip trembles. I've never made it more than a minute with the big vibrator.

"And I'm going to touch myself. You can move everything but your arms. If you stay quiet and don't come before I do, I'll fuck you like you deserve." He drags his hand down to my throat, my collarbone. "So put on a show for me, pet."

I nod. It's all I can do.

He spends a few minutes readying the scene. With my legs now able to move, he removes my jeans and underwear without using the knife. He checks the charge on the massive white wand of the big vibrator, then positions it between my legs, cool against the hot wetness there. These little steps of the ritual drag me ever deeper into this space below myself, where I am just his. Look pretty. Don't make a noise. Don't come. For him.

By the time Dante positions himself on the opposite end of the bed from me, his cock shining, I can barely remember my own name. Just his. It is peaceful and quiet in my mind for the first time in too long to remember.

"Ready?" he asks.

I nod.

With a smile, he flips on the vibrator. "Go."

The firm, bassy vibrations ripple through my system. I squirm, looking for more and less. I can't give into the pleasure they promise. Dante takes himself in hand and begins moving slowly up and down. Another night, I would play with my own breasts, would throw my head back and moan, and would use my whole body to please him. Tonight, I can only rock into and out of the insistent hum, my teeth so deep in my lip I start to taste copper, and hold his gaze.

He starts to pick up speed. "So beautiful for me, pet. So good."

I jerk my hips to the side, slightly dislodging the vibrator. It presses urgently at my entrance, dulled just enough that I might survive this endless task.

He knows me better than I know myself. Dante adjusts the vibrator back into position on my clit without releasing his cock. A whiny moan batters against the prison of my lips, but I won't let it go. I can't. Not when he's so pleased with me.

"I love it when you listen," he groans. "Out in the world, you don't bow down to anybody, but in here you're mine. All mine."

Pleasure reaches warm fingers out for me to take. I could tumble over the edge. I knock the hand away. I am listening to the man I love.

He grunts and stiffens. Hot, white come dribbles over his hand.

"Come for me," he mumbles. "Loud as you can."

My orgasm hits me like a truck, and his name tears from my lips. Aftershocks crash through my body, or is that a second crescendo? The unceasing vibrator pushes me ever higher. When he finally pulls it away, I nearly weep with the loss. That is, until I feel the stiffening head of his cock line up with my entrance. He left me writhing until he was ready again. I open my eyes—when did I close them?—and stare into Dante's as he fucks me hard and fast, wringing yet more pleasure out of me. I wrap my legs around his waist, my hands still clutching the headboard, and when I come again, it's with his sweet praise ringing in my ears.

He knew I could do it. Because he did, so did I.

3 4

SOMETHING TO LOOK
FORWARD TO

Dante

After El falls asleep, I sneak out of bed. Henry might not scare me, but that doesn't mean I don't need to do anything about him. Just that she doesn't need to worry about it.

God, she'd kill me if I ever said that to her face.

This is just a temporary measure, I promise myself as I change in a dark closet and leave the room. *Just until she's no longer pregnant.*

Yeah, that'd stop her from kicking my ass. I shut the bedroom door behind me with a sigh, then call Tony.

He shows up twenty minutes later with Mikey in tow, both of them looking exhausted. I raise an eyebrow.

"Teo needed an angel on his shoulder," Tony says by way of explanation.

"You call in a replacement team?" I ask.

"You think I dropped out of school after kindergarten?" Tony replies.

Mikey just nods and walks in with him. Without conferring, the three of us amble into my office and shut the door behind us. Only

165

once I've poured everybody a drink and sat in the leather chair behind my desk do I begin explaining.

"Wish we'd pruned that branch of the family tree ages ago," Tony mutters when I finish.

"Cheers." I raise my glass to him. "But what the hell do we do?"

"Tony's right." Mikey gestures like snipping a pair of scissors.

Taking Henry out isn't my least favorite option, certainly. This is twice now he's cornered Eleni when she's relaxed, out with Mama, just having a nice time. I'm getting real fucking tired of him trying to use her to piss me off.

And even more tired of it working.

"Are you stupid?" Tony asks. "He's a fucking fed. We drop his ass in the river, and they're crawling all over us like ants before Nonna even gets a chance to kill me for doing it."

"Henry's the only fed I know of looking into us," I say.

"They're like termites." Tony leans back in his chair. "Where you see one, there are a thousand."

"Looking into the Saints?" Mikey raises an eyebrow.

"El said he had a RICO case." I shake my head. "Bastard could be lying."

"We're not kids tagging our first walls," Tony says. "We cover our goddamn tracks. Every other word out of his mouth is a lie, always has been."

I run my finger around the rim of my glass and turn the problem over in my head. The number one thing my father taught me was how to run a clean house. I'm careful enough about taxes that I have three guys for it, and once upon a time, I could point out half the security cameras in the city on a map. Plus, there's a real argument the Saints don't racketeer. I find collecting protection distasteful. No, the only one of us stupid enough to leave a trail was Uncle John.

May he rest in—Hell, let's be honest. I squeeze the arm of the chair he tried to take.

"Let's compromise," I say. "We'll watch him, but we won't bury him 'til he makes a move."

Mikey hums. "And if that's too late?"

Then I've broken a promise to my fiancée and unborn child.

"Then we deal with the consequences." I sigh.

Mikey nods slowly, like he'd make a different choice in my shoes. I look at him out of the corner of my eye. I didn't understand how hard the life he's living is until recently, and he's been married since before I took over the Saints. For all his disappointment pisses me off, I can't help feeling bad for the guy. El's upstairs and something in my chest is trying to escape back to her. I can't imagine leaving her state-lines away.

"Well, since I've got you here," I say, "any other business?"

Tony grimaces. "Raided another Russian spot. Lost three good men, but it's cleared out. Any chance we can put a moratorium on all Kalashnikovs entering the country?"

"Doubtful." I swallow. "Get me their names. I'll allocate the money, make the funeral arrangements."

Tony nods. No one says there hasn't been a raid without a few lost lives, or that the first was Seb. Our numbers are slowly shrinking in the face of this Russian horde, and I'm fucking tired of it. But I can't fix it in the dead of night with my wife—fiancée upstairs.

"Mikey?" I ask.

Mikey's not going to say anything. He never does.

"Actually," Mikey says.

Jesus fuck, the world really is turning inside out. I pin my fickle attention on him and pray he doesn't have more crap news.

"Adri's been talking my ear off for weeks." He sighs. "She'd kill me if I didn't ask you about a date."

"A...date?" I furrow my brow.

"For the wedding." He looks down at his drink. "The wives are planning it."

I didn't even know that. Fuck, I forgot planning a wedding is the next step after proposing. I want to marry El—want it so bad it keeps me awake at night sometimes—but I've been running in so many different directions that the actual marriage part slipped my goddamn mind.

"And you want...what, me to just pick a day?" I ask, trying to get my feet back underneath me.

Mikey shrugs. "Adri'd like that."

Which probably means all the wives have been clawing for information for weeks. Have they picked out a tux for me? Do I get any say in this?

"Tell her to forget it," I mutter. "We'll go to the courthouse. Safer, faster, and I'm not really in a party mood right now."

After tonight, I seriously doubt El is either. She's probably been dozing through these planning meetings.

Mikey exhales through his teeth. "You sure?"

"Yeah?" I frown. "Why not?"

"Cause...." He shakes his head, looks at Tony.

Tony grimaces. He clearly doesn't want to fill in the gaps in Mikey's less than loquacious speech. After a moment of silence, he plunges in anyway.

"Because everything sucks shit right now," he says. "And you love Eleni. She makes you happy. Seeing you be happy would be...good for morale, or whatever."

I grit my teeth and start tallying deaths. Things have been shitty since El and I returned to the city. Tony doesn't make a bad point, as much as it pains him to do so.

"They need something to celebrate," Mikey adds. "Been planning too many funerals."

At the beginning of the summer, before Eleni, I would've seen that myself.

"Okay," I say. "I'll pick a date."

3 5

BAD FEELING

ELENI

THE NEXT MORNING, my vibrating phone wakes me before my alarm. I shoot up in bed, immediately certain Dante snuck out, that he's captured or bleeding out at Henry's feet.

He lays in bed next to me, his dark hair rumpled. As I watch, he rolls over to reveal a dent from the pillowcase in his cheek. I exhale slowly and pick up my phone.

Mama's calling. I glance at Dante one last time, then grab a robe and pad out into the hallway.

"Hi, Mama," I say.

"I am very disappointed," she says severely.

I rub my eyes, check the time. It's barely six-thirty. What could I have done already?

"I told you I was going out to Staten Island," I say.

"Pah." She huffs a breath. "You think I'm worried about that? No, *zouzouni*, I want to know why I just had to find out the date of your wedding from some *woman*"—she says the word like it's poison—

169

"showing up at the door to ask you about something called a save-the-date. Am I not your mama anymore?"

"What?" I freeze at the top of the stairs. "We don't have a date for the wedding. What woman?"

Mama rattles off a description that matches Nicky to a T, down to the suit. "She seemed very confident, *zouzouni*. She said Dante picked it out."

So, not some ghost of Camila, returned to torture me. That's great.

"Uh, you didn't hear from me because I heard it from you," I reply. "When did she say?"

"Next weekend." The edge leaks out of Mama's voice. "You really didn't know?"

"Nope. I don't even know when Dante would've—" Dimly, I remember the mattress shifting in the dead of night. I assumed he just needed to go to the bathroom. Was he meeting with someone? "Sorry, Mama, I would've told you if I'd known."

"I'm sorry too." She sighs. "I should've known. You are under so much pressure, but you wouldn't forget your mama."

Pressure's one word for it. I continue down the stairs to make one of the million identical herbal teas I have to drink now instead of coffee. "Of course not. What did you tell Nicky?"

"That you would call her after your very important classes."

"Thanks," I say, but my voice is dull even to my own ears.

"What is it? Do you not like the date?" Mama asks.

"No, I—" I start the kettle and lean against the counter, staring at the kitchen that holds so many of my memories. "I don't know, I'm looking forward to being his wife, but with everything going on right now, a wedding just seems…silly."

Mama scoffs. "There's nothing silly about a wedding. You'll remember it for the rest of your lives. And if everything is so 'going on,' then do you not deserve a chance to stand up in front of your loved ones and tell them how much you love each other?"

I smile. "You just don't want your first grandchild born in sin."

"I will have that if I drive you to the courthouse myself," Mama says stubbornly. "You are thinking about too much. It's not good for baby."

Both of us make the spitting noise in unison, and I smile.

"Take Dante away from his work for a day. Spend it together. Stop your worrying," Mama says. "Or I will make you."

Her threat rings true. I have one midterm today, but then the rest of my classes are basically just study periods. It wouldn't be hard to blow off the rest of the day and spend it with Dante. That is, if I can pull him away from his worrying.

"Thanks, Mama," I say. "And I'm sorry about Nicky."

"Stop that." I can picture her shaking her head. "Be happy, *zouzouni*, and make me happy."

I hang up with my mind whirling. By the time Dante wanders down, I've over-steeped my tea and brewed a new cup. His pajama pants hang low on his waist, exposing a tantalizing V of muscles, and I wonder for a moment if I could forge a doctor's note good enough to make up my midterm.

"What are you thinking?" He smiles as he starts the coffee pot. "If you're worrying about getting to class, I'm happy to drive."

I shake my head. "About us."

He sucks in a breath. "I should tell you something. Last night—"

I put up a hand, and he stops.

"Is this about the wedding?"

He nods.

"Mama called to yell at me for not telling her."

He winces. "I'm so sorry. Mikey dragged an answer out of me last night, and I forgot to tell him not to tell Adri until the morning."

I shake my head and smile. "It's okay. She responded better when she realized I didn't know."

"Thank God." He sits on a stool. "What do you think about the date? Is next Saturday too soon?"

I blow out a long breath. "It's definitely soon. But I kind of feel like there's no point in wasting time."

"Exactly!" Dante grins. "I asked Mikey the earliest he thought the wives could have it together. I'm tired of calling you my fiancée."

My chest warms, and I fidget with the mug of tea I don't really want to drink. "With that…do you think we could spend some time alone together this week? Like, maybe out here?"

I didn't intend to add that last part. When Dante's eyebrows flick up in surprise, I know I've made a mistake.

"Is this about Henry?" he asks slowly.

I shake my head. "Not really. It's just about everything. I feel like we're both running in a million different directions. I just woke up next to you, and I miss you." I run my hand over my stomach. "We miss you."

Dante hops off his stool and wraps me in a hug. "I'm right here, El. Or wherever else you want me. Always."

I nod against his skin. Like this, a wedding doesn't seem so silly at all.

"But I have to ask," he says. "You've been wanting to be out here a lot lately. Any reason why?"

In the safe harbor of his arms, everything pours out. "I feel like I have everything I've ever dreamed of, but it's like the pieces of a dozen different jigsaws. The Tandon pieces don't match the Saints pieces, the baby pieces don't match the city ones, and every time I feel like I've figured out what someone wants me to be, I'm suddenly somewhere else and they want another person entirely."

Dante squeezes me tighter. "Do you know what puzzles you want to finish?"

After a long minute, I nod. "The one with you and me and baby."

"Nothing else?" There's a soft note of surprise in his voice.

"Maybe not." I slump against him, weak with relief. I finally said it. I worked so hard for a life I don't know that I want. Maybe that's not the worst thing in the world. Maybe I can work just as hard to change it.

He kisses the side of my head. "How about we get dressed, I drive you to school, and then I pick you up after your midterm and we talk more?"

I pull back and grin at him. "That sounds perfect."

He swats my ass lightly. "Then get going."

I scurry upstairs and dress quickly. Armando will bring my books from the apartment. Just one midterm, and then Dante and I can figure out our lives.

When I come back down, I hear voices in the kitchen. Is somebody here? I creep down the hall, just in case, and see Dante on the phone.

"Wait for me." He sighs. "I know, just fucking wait!"

He hangs up.

"Dante?" I ask.

His body tenses. Then, he turns to me slowly. "Saints piece. Leo's going to drive you in, but I promise I'll pick you up." He grabs my hand, kisses it, and marches past me up the stairs.

I've got a bad feeling he's not going to keep that promise.

3 6

BRIGADIER

Dante

I WALK UP to a shuttered bodega. Pieces of the paper sign flap in the wind, declaring that I can get "sacks" and "dinks" inside. New York City flows around this abandoned piece of itself, not even glancing at it.

Perfect.

I slide into the alley beside it, unlock the chain on the back door, and step inside. Tony and Cal Duncan stand in the flickering light of the ex-backroom, now lined with knives, cattle prods, ropes, and any other torture instrument a Saint has come up with in the last decade.

"I was wondering if you'd ever show your fine face." Cal smiles. "I called you as soon as I heard."

"I had other business," I answer crisply. "What did you catch?"

"A tuna, if I do say so myself."

Tony rolls his eyes. "Brigadier. No sign of Fyodor, but the place was obviously important to them."

Someone grunts just past the thin door that separates us from the main room. I smile. Brigadier means decent information.

175

"Who has him?" I ask.

"One of my boys wanted first touch." Cal grins. "Simply a softening job, nary a question asked. Don't you worry." He winks.

There are a lot of things I'd rather die than trust an Irish King with. Torture isn't one of them. I nod easily.

"And our cousin?" I ask Tony.

Cal's smile fades a degree. "Now, there's no need for secrets between friends."

"Safe with Uncle Patterson," Tony replies.

Which means Teo not only survived whatever encounter Cal had with the Russians but has already been squirreled back to Patterson with Mikey. I crack my knuckles.

"Then let's get to work."

The three of us stride into the main abandoned bodega space. Over the newspapers that look to be covering the windows from the front, thick mats of ridged foam dampen any sound that could escape to the outside. Cal's boys have all the lights blaring, giving the middle-aged man tied to the chair in the middle of the room nowhere to hide. His pale, bare chest shows thick lines of red between a tapestry of tattoos, and a wild-eyed redhead in the middle of the room holds an equally crimson knife.

"Just one more," the redhead says, not looking away from his prey. "He's gas for yelling."

Cal clicks his tongue. "Really? I'm not one minute through the door, and you ask this?"

The redhead jumps as if snapping back into himself, sets the knife down on the counter, and backs up to stand with a few other Kings along the walls. Thankfully, they're matched one for one by Saints' men.

With me, we have the numbers.

"All yours." Cal bows dramatically.

I pull off my jacket and pull on the heavy butcher's apron that's hung here for as long as I can remember. "Brigadier have a name?"

"*Khuy tebe*," he hisses.

"Wordy." I wander over to the counter and survey the implements.

At least a dozen different knives. Creativity, the Kings seem to lack. I select a solid iron pipe. "Can I call you Teb?"

"*Nye—*"

I swing the pipe into his shredded chest, and Teb chokes on his answer.

"*No* isn't an option for you any longer." I smile. "Forgot to mention that."

He spits blood on the floor and mutters something in Russian I don't catch.

"I'm looking for a friend of mine." I twirl the pipe. "You may have heard of him. Fyodor?"

Teb starts to laugh, and I crack the pipe into his shoulder. Something breaks, and he shouts in pain.

"Where is he?"

Tony sets his hands on Teb's shoulders, massaging the destroyed one. I smile.

Teb grits his teeth. "Hit me, cut me, I will not talk."

"We'll see about that." I wander away from him. Russians tend to be tough, but that only means I need something unique. I pluck an electrified cattle prod off the counter and keep my body between it and him. Time to see how he likes a little surprise.

"Fyodor," I repeat. "Where can I find him?"

Tony shifts out of the way, anticipating my move.

Teb spits. "You know so little. You do not even know what you had, when you had Camila. You will fail."

"I will?" I jab the cattle prod into his back, right where the electricity should reach his kidneys.

He spasms with another yell. I pull the prod back after long seconds of twitching muscles. He slumps against the chair, and Tony laughs.

I hum thoughtfully. "I *thought* Camila was a bitch who'd fuck her way to the top at a moment's notice. Was I wrong?"

Teb laughs breathlessly. "That, she is. But she was Fyodor's bitch, until she wasn't."

"And that's why she wanted me so bad." I run the prod softly across his bare back, setting off a series of miniature shocks. "See, talking isn't so bad."

"About dead bitches? No." He bares his teeth. "Nothing more."

El's class is only two hours long. I'd love to take my time with this bastard, break him down piece by piece, but I can't be late. I can't break a promise to her. So I look to Tony, and then to Cal.

"Well?" I ask. "You want a piece, or what?"

I swear to God, Cal drools.

AN HOUR AND A HALF LATER, Teb lays on the floor, his chair broken. The zip cuffs holding him in place are barely attached to anything anymore, but he doesn't have the strength to move his head away from the slowly spreading puddle of his own puke, much less get up and run out.

I squat next to him. "Hey. Remember me?"

His swollen eyelids flutter.

"I'll take that as a yes. You want to die?"

For that, he manages a nod.

"Impressive." I grin. "We'll kill you if you answer a couple simple questions. That sound good?"

Another nod.

"Where is Fyodor?"

"Don't...know...." Teb mumbles through bloody lips and several broken teeth.

Cal rears back with the claw hammer he apparently favors, but I put up a hand. Teb's got maybe one hit left in him before unconsciousness, and I'm not wasting it on Cal Duncan's temper.

Or my own. I'm cutting it very close to being late.

"What do you know about him?" I ask.

"His movements," Tony adds. "His plans. Who he started spending time with after Camila."

A gob of blood drizzles out of Teb's mouth. For a moment, I think we've lost him. Then, he coughs, and another tooth shard scatters across the floor.

"His plans are…you," Teb says. "You have… *krysa.*"

I glance up at Cal, Tony. Both of them look equally confused.

"Translate that," I bark.

Nothing. I nudge Teb with my foot. His eyelids don't even move. Fuck.

"Wrap him up," I tell Tony. "Keep him alive somewhere. I don't give a shit where."

Then, I begin furiously yanking off the gloves I donned when things got messy. I need my fucking phone, I need to figure out what he said before I forget it. The thick, black rubber slaps to the wet floor.

My fingers fumble over the screen. English sounds don't translate well to Cyrillic, but I get there with a flash of ice over my skin.

"Rat," I whisper. "He said we have a goddamn rat!"

I storm out of the room without looking behind me, ripping off the apron as I go. His plans are me, and I have a fucking rat. That means it doesn't matter how many guards I have on Eleni, I won't be able to breathe until I'm looking at her again.

3 7

ADAPTATION

Eleni

I WALK OUT OF TANDON, my hands sore from furiously typing for the last two hours, and blink in the sunlight. No sign of Dante. My stomach sinks.

"Have you heard from him?" I ask Armando.

He shakes his head. I reach for my phone.

And a slick, black coupe pulls up in front of the school. The window buzzes down to reveal Dante inside. In unison, we sigh.

"Wait, why were you worried?" I ask.

He glances around. "I'll explain later. You ready for our day?"

I look at the tiny car, then at the guards.

"They'll follow behind." Dante smiles. "Come on."

I've never been able to say no to that smile.

I DON'T KNOW what I expected when I asked to spend the day with Dante, but I didn't expect this. It's a little like the day I first visited the

Tandon registrar. We wander the city, shopping aimlessly. Intentionally aimlessly, I realize, like Dante's trying to create a path no one can follow. Though that sends cold fingers of worry up my spine, I try to just enjoy him. We eat a long, late lunch. We register at random places for the wedding. A kitchen and bath store. A sex toy store, because they offer the option and it's too funny not to. A furniture store. It really looks like we're building a life together, not like we already have one.

Hand-in-hand, we walk past a baby store. My feet pause.

"El?" he asks.

"Is it safe to go in?" I murmur. "Or…?"

I don't need to ask if we're being watched. By the tension in Dante's shoulders, I already know. Something changed between that phone call and when he picked me up. I start to hurry on down the street, sick to my stomach with something other than pregnancy for the first time in a long time.

"No, wait." He doesn't move.

I pause.

His jaw works. "If it's not safe to go in, then it's already not safe to be pregnant."

I make the spitting noise.

"We can't have a baby with no things." He offers me a forced smile.

Somehow, this isn't how I expected our first baby shopping to go. But I walk inside with him.

The store unfolds in a patchwork of pastels. Cribs over there, playpens on the other side, and an absolute treasure trove of the tiniest toys and clothes I've ever seen in the middle. Tears sting my eyes as I drift up to an itty pair of sneakers. There are babies who wear these. Safe babies, who squirm as their mamas try to fit their fat little feet into faux leather and false laces. I don't even know what sex Baby is. I don't know anything.

Dante's hand is suddenly warm on the small of my back. "You think they'll be sporty?"

"I think they'll be scared," I whisper.

His hand tenses. I've shattered the fiction of this day.

"No," he says roughly.

I look up at him, the hard planes of his face, the slash of his mouth.

"Can we really leave?" I ask before I can stop myself.

He sighs. "I—"

"I was looking at the documents." I run my fingers over the tiny sneakers. "Just trying to get a sense of the business. There's a Saints outpost in Brindisi, on the east coast of Italy, isn't there?"

"We can't talk about this here." He glances around. "I made us reservations with an old friend of mine. Can you wait until dinner?"

No. I'm bursting at the seams. But I pull the sneakers off the rack. "I can if we buy these."

The smile that blooms across his face is tired but honest. "Always."

THE SKY IS red and purple with sunset, and I'm feeling beautiful in a new, sapphire-colored dress with an empire waist to hide my swelling stomach by the time Dante leads me up a few stairs to his "old friend's" place. A burly bouncer stands at the door.

"Reservation?" he says.

"Cattaneo," Dante replies. "Standing table."

The bouncer looks the two of us over, nods, and unhooks a velvet rope to let us into what really seems like just another brownstone.

"Giancarlo is a wizard," Dante says as we walk in. "He can do things with pasta you can't even imagine, but he has the worst authority problems I've ever seen. So he runs a less-than-legal restaurant out of his home. Perfect privacy."

I laugh. Of course, this is where a mafioso takes his fiancée on a date. At least my laughter makes Dante smile.

Up the few steps, a waiter in all black welcomes us into a warm-toned living room. Beyond it, I can see three small tables, all curtained away from each other and open to the state-of-the-art kitchen. The waiter leads us to one, tells us brusquely this isn't the sort of place with menus, and starts to turn away.

"No swordfish," Dante declares. "Marlin or mackerel either. Nothing raw or unpasteurized."

The waiter makes a face like Dante's just pissed on his leg, but he nods and hurries away. Dante pulls out a chair for me, and I sit. There's a low hum of conversation in the room, but I don't know how many—if any—of the tables are occupied.

It's perfect.

"So, Brindisi," Dante says. "Why there?"

I swallow. "I was just looking, but…there's a ferry there. It goes straight between Greece and Italy, every day."

He smiles. "That ferry ride takes about eight hours. It's a two-and-a-half-hour flight."

"You've been checking?"

"I've been thinking." He sighs. "It's hard not to."

"Because of what happened earlier?" I peek up at him.

He laughs. "I can't keep shit from you, huh?"

I shake my head.

"Good." His smile lingers after his laughter stops. "We caught a Russian brigadier, and he said we had a rat."

My stomach drops to my toes just as the sour waiter arrives with two tiny glasses of something clear.

"Aperitif," he says.

Dante knocks them both back as soon as he leaves. A moment later, a portly man in a white coat steps into the kitchen. Giancarlo, probably. Classical music pours from invisible speakers, and he begins cooking.

"Do you believe him?" I whisper.

"I have to." Dante looks grim. "Apparently, Fyodor's chasing me, too."

I put my hand on my stomach and try not to panic.

"If we left," Dante says, "what about Tandon?"

I shake my head. "Mama mentioned a school called NTU, in Athens. Apparently, it's very good for computer engineering."

"Athens is a six-hour direct flight from Brindisi." Dante twists his empty glass thoughtfully.

The word "rat" vibrates through my mind. I spit mentally, protecting Baby however I can. I should start carrying a gun again.

"Everything is different now," I murmur.

"Do you want to leave?" he asks for the first time in a long time. "I can send you away tonight. Parikia, Athens, Oklahoma, wherever you want."

My heart hammers against my rib cage. "No!"

Giancarlo glances up at me with a scowl. I lower my voice.

"Look, you were right in the beginning," I say urgently. "I should've left. But it's too late now."

"It's never—"

I shake my head, fighting to express the panic that rose up in me at the idea of leaving.

"I can't go anywhere without you," I say simply. "If you want out, I'll go. We can run the operation in Brindisi, or start a new operation, or become farmers. If you want to stay, I'll learn how to adapt. But I'm yours, Dante. I have been since the virginity auction. Tell me where to be so I can stop trying to be everywhere."

Giancarlo claps, and the waiter comes around with plates of a steaming, mushroom-heavy appetizer. Dante looks from the plate to me, then takes my hand and squeezes it.

"I don't make decisions without you anymore," he says.

38

BOUND TOGETHER

Dante

Dinner at Giancarlo's is spectacular, as always, but I can't think about anything other than the look on Eleni's face when she asked me to tell her where to go. Who to be. I've seen that look a thousand times, on a thousand different women. Even on El, when I've pushed her to her limits in bed. Once upon a time, I thought it was all I wanted in a partner. To be submissive, pliant, able to fit into my world. Hell, I used to think that was what I wanted out of Eleni.

But things have changed, she's right. She's just wrong about when. Everything changed the moment she told me why to get a gyro. Again when I took her to bed. A third time when I came back from being shot and discovered she'd whipped my crew into shape. Maybe I used to be a Dante who would've taken that open request for an answer and written my own will onto it. I can't anymore. Not with her.

We drive back to the house on Staten Island in silence. El's still quiet as we walk inside, past the guards.

"Go to the bedroom," I say once the door closes behind us.

El's shoulders slump with the ease of submission, and she obeys

187

immediately. I smile as I follow her up the stairs. She's always testing my rules, but never when I expect.

"Undress." I step into the bedroom and begin doing the same.

Clothes rain off us. She's naked in seconds, and it takes every bit of willpower I have to remember my plan, to not just fall to my knees and begin worshipping her. Her breasts are starting to swell, and the soft roundness of her stomach is intoxicating.

"On the bed." I turn away to grab a few lengths of rope.

When I turn back, El lays spread eagle, already reaching for the bedposts. My cock stiffens, but I focus. She needs me tonight.

I start with the easy work. My left ankle to her right. Tying the knots is meditative, and I usually allow her to slip into sub-space while I do it. Tonight, I explain.

"You're trapped between too many answers."

She nods.

"But I won't make our lives without you." I kiss her knee.

"Please?" she says plaintively. "I'm yours."

I shake my head. "No more than I'm yours. That's why we're getting married. I need the world to know that there is no me without you anymore."

A tear slips down her cheek. I tighten the final knot and crawl up her body.

"So I'm going to prove it to you." I thread the second length of rope around my right wrist and her left. "Far fewer choices. But tonight, we don't move without each other."

More tears drip down her perfect face, and I start to worry. "Color?"

She sniffles. "Gr-green."

"Good." I kiss her salt-stained cheek. "You'll tell me if that changes."

She nods.

I tug the rope with my teeth, and the bindings are done. Hand to hand, foot to foot, we lay there for a long moment. Just feeling her skin sends blood rushing for my cock, but I'm happy to wait for her. Always.

"Move our hands when you're ready, pet," I say. "Wherever you want them."

Another long moment of quiet passes. Then, with the tug of rope, she slides our hands down between us and cups my cock. I slide my fingers between her legs and find the first droplets of wetness there.

She shakes her head. "You first. Both of us."

I smile. "And my mouth?"

"Yours," she says. "I only have your hand."

Little pedant. But fine. I palm my cock, buck up into the warm pressure of both of us, then lower my lips to her neck.

Slowly, she starts moving along my length. I kiss her at the same speed, dragging my tongue along her skin. When she speeds up, so do I. With small nips, I tease her.

"Bite me," she gasps.

"The wedding," I remind her.

"I thought I was making decisions," she snaps back.

There's my El. I sink my teeth into the place where her neck meets her shoulder and suck a dark bruise. Her other hand slides between us to cup my balls, and I jerk, nearly overwhelmed already. I want this to last, but who am I to refuse her tonight?

I ring her throat with bruises like a black pearl necklace as she coaxes me over the edge one slow stroke at a time. Sticky warmth splatters between us, and I groan her name. A glimpse of her smile, over the edge of her chin, sneaks into my vision.

Before I'm truly back in my body again, El is already guiding our hands inexorably to her pussy. I thank God I can fuck her half out of my mind at this point and find her clit without looking. She arches up into me, and a slick sound tells me she's entered herself. Two fingers, judging by the way she moans. The tug of the rope as she fucks herself throws off my rhythm, and I wouldn't have it any other way. We move like two parts of the same body, inescapably together. I drop my mouth to her swollen breasts and decorate the tops with more bruises before pulling a sweet, taut nipple into my mouth. Curse words drop from her lips like jewels in that old story, and I feel her start to shake.

"Perfect," I murmur against her skin. "Beautiful. You can take more."

A high, delighted laugh breaks into her moans. "Bossy."

"Always." I roll her nipple between my teeth.

With my tied ankle, I spread her legs wider. We work together, which means we both get our say sometimes, and right now, I want to fucking hear her. Her third finger slips into place past my hand.

Wet sounds echo through the room. I groan, and new blood shoots to my spent cock. She grinds up into me. Her trembling intensifies. I press my free hand to the skin of her abdomen, just above her hips, maximizing the pleasure of her fingers inside her, and she comes with a shout.

I lick and suck at her breasts through the aftershocks, murmuring more soft compliments against her skin. Finally, she pulls her hand out of herself. I put my free hand on the bed and push up to see her face. If she's tired, we can stop now. I'll handle my achingly-hard cock and enjoy spoiling her for the rest of the night.

There is no sign of the silent Eleni I rode home with in her face. She is so alive, her blue eyes on fire, her mouth hungry and red. Before I can say a word, she is lining up my cock with her entrance. I smile and thrust into her.

She flings our combined hands up, against the pillows, out of the way. The loss of control is potent and strange, unlike anything I've ever felt before. A tempting haze of release sneaks through my brain.

Is this what it feels like to submit? Is this why people like it?

El threads her other hand into my hair like a desperate anchor, and the thought flees my mind. I am hers, like I said, and nothing else matters. So if she wants my cock, she'll have it.

I fuck her into the mattress, my hips perfect pistons, meeting her clit with my wiry pubic hair every time. El moans, writhes, starts to fall apart. I just watch. I don't even need my hands to turn her into a ruin. She knew that already.

That tightens something in my gut, and I know my second orgasm is coming quickly. I focus on moving with her, chasing the rhythm of her hips. They jerk, twist with the promise she's not far behind.

"Together," I say.

She nods. "Together."

Staring into the face of the woman I love, feeling every inch of her around me, struggling against the tug of the ropes, it doesn't take any more for my brain to go white with pleasure. She tightens with a scream as she follows me.

Together.

39

───────

MORNING OF

"BWAH! BWAH! BWAH!"

The screaming alarm—alarms—rip me out of sleep far too early. I grope for the nearest one, which turns out to be my phone, and silence it before even opening my eyes. Another keeps whining somewhere else in the room, and I groan.

Last night is a blur of strobe lights, penis-shaped candy, and mob wives dancing like drunk sorority girls. As much as I'm going to kill whoever set all these alarms, at least my no-drinking rule means it's only regular awful, not hungover awful.

Another groan answers mine, and I shoot upright.

I'm—where the fuck am I? Big, soft bed. Early morning light in the window. It's shaped like the Staten Island house, but the colors—pink walls, purple bedspread, rainbow throw pillows....

The second groan issues from the floor again, and I glance over the edge. Gianna lies there, makeup smeared across her face and hair falling out of the updo she slaved over last night. She looks distinctly green.

"Kill it," she mumbles. "With fire."

I'm in her room at the Staten Island house. And I'm getting married today, so someone—probably Mama—set every alarm in the house to make sure we got up on time. I scan the bedroom and spot her phone, wedged half under the dresser. Gotcha! I stand—legs a little sore after all that dancing, but steady—and cross the room to shut off the alarm. Gianna sighs in relief.

"I thought the maid of honor was supposed to take care of the bride." I squat down next to her.

"Get married another day." She flaps her hand at me. "You don't give a fuck."

I don't, really, but all the planning is done, and I'm not going to piss off Nicky by throwing that away. And there's an elderly priest waiting for us at a nearby Catholic church.

With a smile, I help Gianna off the floor, hold her hair back while she pukes, then strip her out of last night's dress and stuff her in a cold shower. When it seems like she's not going to drown, I pull on a robe and head to the kitchen.

The smell of loukoumades nearly lifts me off my feet like a cartoon character. I float in to find Mama at the stove. More alarms blare upstairs.

"Morning," I say over the noise.

"*Zouzouni!*" Mama whips around, abandoning her food for one of the first times ever, and bursts into tears. "You look so beautiful."

I look and feel like roadkill, though I collapsed out of exhaustion rather than drunkenness, but I accept her hug until something starts smelling like smoke. Mama swears in Greek, pats my cheek, and turns back just in time for the smoke alarm to add its opinions to the cacophony. The doorbell rings.

And I start laughing. It's beyond the pale that I'm getting married today. That Nicky planned the ceremony, so we're going to a Catholic church instead of Greek Orthodox like I know Mama wants. That I'm going to pose for first-look pictures with Dante while both of us wonder which of our guests is giving up all our secrets.

Gianna stumbles out of the bathroom, drenched. "Do you hate me?"

~

WE MANAGE to silence the alarms and salvage most of the batch of loukoumades. The doorbell turns out to be a makeup team nobody warned me about. They hustle me into the den, which somebody told them would be their headquarters. Four members of the six-person team begin shifting furniture out of the way, a fifth sets up a long table in the middle, and the sixth, a platinum-blonde woman who looks like a fox, studies my face.

"Puffy," she says. "Lovely eyes. Your mother said you wanted bombshell, yes?"

I don't even think Mama knows the word bombshell. "Did you talk to a woman named Nicky?"

She nods.

"That's not my mother," I say. "I want more natural."

The fox-faced woman sighs.

Then, the whirlwind really begins. I'm changed into a white silk robe. More wives begin arriving. Nicky, apparently, is already at the church. Mama makes a face every time the church comes up, but she still hasn't said anything. The fox-faced woman powders, plucks, shaves, and prunes me before passing me off down the line. Another of her army winds my hair in a complex updo while Val studies the work and reports its progress to Nicky over the phone. I laugh as Gianna tries to politely refuse a glass of champagne that makes her turn green.

Someone tells me that the tailor will be dropping off my dress soon. This will be the first time I've seen it.

By the time I've made it almost all the way around the table, back to the fox-faced woman for hopefully final approval, I can't stop thinking about the fact I haven't seen Dante since Friday morning. I expected to have a last night with him, before my bachelorette party on Saturday, but Mama and Gianna picked me up in a limo and dragged me out to Staten Island for the spa night before the lazy day before the party before my wedding. No men allowed.

I slip my phone out of the pocket of my robe and send him a quick text, asking if he feels like a factory sausage too.

"Ah-ah!" Mama snatches my phone. "No distractions for the bride."

"But—"

She shakes her finger at me, happy tears in her eyes again. At least if Dante's set-up is anything like mine, he won't be able to answer me, so I'm not missing much.

The final makeup artist passes me back to the fox-faced woman. She smears something below my bottom lip, adds a few more sprinkles of glitter to my cheeks, then claps. I jump.

Two of her army—two more? There are already five around the table—hurry in with a white garment bag. That has to be the dress.

"Who's going to help her?" the fox-faced woman barks. "You can't ruin the hair and makeup."

"I will," Mama says.

Every eye in the room turns to Gianna, even mine. She winces apologetically and shakes her head. Way too sick.

That's fine. This is all for show anyway.

I step behind an accordioning, painted wall the fox-faced woman's army put up with Mama. She hangs the dress over the back and unzips the bag.

Suddenly, I can't look. I twist and face the mirror instead, then shut my eyes before I absorb any details of my hair or makeup.

"Are you wearing the right underwear, *zouzouni?*" she asks.

"Robe off, hands up." Fabric rustles behind me.

I obey. A few days ago, a set of lacy white lingerie arrived. The idea of wearing sexy underwear someone else picked out for me immediately made me sick, so the only thing I've bought for this wedding is that. Practically, I picked a set with a corset to hide any baby bump. Rebelliously, I got it in bright red.

Something light and airy settles over my head. Mama tugs a few times before it settles into place, zips up the back, then sucks in a watery breath. "Oh, Eleni."

I open my eyes. The woman in the mirror barely looks like me. My untamable curls twist neatly together in a complex bun, clearly just waiting for a veil. Despite her displeasure, the fox-faced woman has given me a fairly natural makeup look—a soft, smokey eye, a nearly nude lip, heaps of golden glitter that manage not to look like something Gianna would wear to work. And the dress...based on Mama's expression, she hasn't seen it before, so this has to be Gianna's doing. The sleeves reach my wrists and drape away to the floor, a concession to the season, but they're lace all the way to the shoulder, baring miles of skin. The skirt is the opposite of the cupcake I feared, a sleek A-line that won't trip me up, but it has its own separate train made from the same lace as the sleeves. The top echoes the camisole we picked out together so long ago, a sweetheart neckline, and it has enough structure that I probably didn't need the corset.

Mama adds a simple veil, attached to a tiny tiara studded with sapphires that bring out my eyes. Then, almost sheepishly, she offers me a wrinkled, dried, deep red Greek peony.

"A silly American tradition," she says. "But you still need your 'something borrowed.' This is the last flower I have left from my wedding to Baba."

My breath catches. "Thank you, Mama."

She reveals a small clip on the back, clearly attached recently, and attaches it to my hair. I look in the mirror one last time.

Holy shit, I'm getting married.

Mrs. Cattaneo, here I come!

40

WEDDING BELLS

Dante

I STRETCH my sore knuckles on the little stage that holds the altar at St. Michael's, a church I haven't set foot inside since Mom died. As Dad used to say, church is for people who confess their sins, and Saints aren't that goddamn stupid.

But it seems like I am. Father Stefan's gaze follows the movement of my hands and snags on my split, bruised knuckles. He frowns. I thank God they built this church with the organ so close to the front that he couldn't nag me about them if he wanted to. He'd probably start with how many masses I've missed anyway.

God hasn't struck me with lighting yet, but Fyodor seems well on his way to trying, so I'll take my chances.

The doors open, and I jerk my head up, hoping for El. Fuck, I've missed her.

No dice. Tony and Gianna enter, arm in arm. Tony wears the same deep purple suit I do, with the same sprig of greenish flowers pinned to his lapel, but he manages to look a little less uncomfortable. Gianna looks like death warmed over in a floor-length, forest green cocktail dress. I don't think it's the dress's fault. No, I'd guess El actually had the blow-out, kiss-the-single-life-goodbye party that I didn't have time for in two full days standing in an abandoned bodega, beating the shit out of Teb, and her maid of honor is feeling the consequences.

I look out over the crowded pews and wish I recognized more of the faces. This is the problem with a Sunday wedding. The whole congregation is here, from babies to old men and women clutching walkers to balance through the long procession. Our guests dot the crowd, sticking out like sore thumbs. Pitch-black suits amidst the grays and browns and blues. Neon-colored dresses between soft florals and woven hats. But that doesn't mean the rat Teb mentioned couldn't have snuck in, hidden somewhere in all those regular faces.

Two fucking days, and we didn't get another useful word out of the bastard. At least outside of church, my failures don't still count as sins.

Maybe I should watch my tongue. There's still a chance for God to strike me down. Adri stands in one of the front pews, holding ten-year-old Mona's hand while sixteen-year-old Al watches the doors. No sign of Mikey yet, which means he's still dumping Teb's body. Maybe God has a sense of humor, and he's waiting until the deed is properly done.

I flex my aching hands again. Tony and Gianna reach the altar, split. Tony comes to stand by me, and we exchange a look. I know his knuckles aren't in a much better state. I also know he's thinking about blowing off the reception to go find out what Cal dug up in our absence. I haven't decided if I give a shit yet.

When I told Cal I had to go, he was pissed. Demanded to know what the fuck was more important than finding this bastard. With five of his guys in the room, I couldn't throw my wedding in his face like I wanted to. Inviting Cal—and I know he would demand an invitation—would be one thing. A whole pack of Irish Kings was another entirely. So I just told him that he agreed I could be the fucking boss, which meant I left when I said I had to leave, and then ordered him to keep chasing the lead of whoever the hell Fyodor is sleeping with now.

Hopefully, he comes up with something. Then, I won't have

wasted my last night with El before our wedding on a few bruises and nothing more. I'm getting real fucking tired of chasing a ghost.

Bridesmaids and groomsmen seem to keep appearing forever. I swear, people start walking in that I don't recognize. Mikey arrives and hurries down to the front. From a side entrance, two more men in suits that I actually don't recognize hurry inside and take a pew in the back.

The hairs on the back of my neck raise. Who the fuck are they? Every man I have in this church is armed to the teeth, just in case Fyodor thinks this is his moment, so I'm not worried about two dick-heads, but that doesn't mean I'm itching for a firefight at my goddamn wedding. I glance at the little nook with the stained-glass window of St. Nicholas, where a velvet kneeler hides enough guns for even this endless parade of groomsmen.

The hymn swells, and the main doors open again. Before I even look up, I know. El's finally here.

I meet her eyes down the aisle.

Instantly, I forget about everything outside of St. Michael's and most of the things inside it. There's no room for anything in my brain but her. She's stunning. Awe-inspiring. Something beyond that. Her dress strides the line between sexy and way-too-sexy for church. The glimpses of her arms through the long sleeves are strangely tantalizing, even pulling my gaze away from the truly impressive cleavage bubbling from the neckline. I can't see the back from here, but I begin praying for a zipper.

This is what the wedding's really about. Not the stuffed pews, not the hymns, not Father Stefan's wheezy homily. Making this beautiful woman my wife, and then taking her home to fuck the absolute shit out of her.

I don't realize she's arm-in-arm with Mama until they reach the foot of the little stage. Mama offers me Eleni's hand.

"I don't need to say it, do I?" she asks.

I shake my head. She's made her various threats more than clear, which I appreciate. With a small smile, Mama puts El's hand in mine and takes a seat in the front pew. Father Stefan raises his hands and begins the greeting, but I only have eyes for Eleni.

She grins at me through the lace of her veil. I'd give almost anything to rip it off her without waiting a full mass. My wife, very nearly. Her smile fades a little as she glances at the pews, and I realize she's just as uncomfortable being here, in front of all these people, as I am. I take her hand, then start tracing surreptitious letters on her palm.

When I reach the end of *elope instead*, her smile returns. And for that, I'll wear the fucking purple suit and listen to the readings and stand here until my knees give out.

Finally, Father Stefan reaches the important parts. I nod along through all the "do yous," knowing I'll do anything for this woman. For worse? Check. In sickness? Already done. Poorer? Well, I doubt I'll ever have to prove that one, but I'd live with El in a cardboard box if she wanted to.

"I do," I say, proud and certain.

When El's turn comes, her voice wobbles with tears. I grin. We didn't have time for writing our own vows, but this is just as good.

Father Stefan blesses the rings, then hands hers to me. I went back to Louie for it almost as soon as she said yes, so the craftwork is incredible. Unlike the bold, distinct bands of gold and silver in her engagement ring, here the two metals are twined so closely together they almost look like wire, layered over itself a hundred times. An interlinked net of our lives, now impossible to pull apart.

"With this ring, I thee wed," I say.

She smiles down at it for a moment. It fits perfectly, both on her finger and against the other one. Then, she takes my ring, which I've felt naked without all day.

"With this ring, I thee wed." She starts to put it on my thumb, a reminder of how long she wore it, then shifts to my ring finger when Father Stefan sighs.

"You may now kiss the bride," he says.

I throw back her veil, and though she's made up like a Broadway performer, she's still my El. I couldn't imagine her being anyone else.

When I kiss her soundly, only half aware of all those kids I saw in the audience, my mind drifts thankfully to the fact that we made it through the ceremony without gunfire.

Rare, for mafia weddings, but I will absolutely take it.

Once Father Stefan finishes his endless mass, I pick up my beaming wife and carry her out of the church, into the rest of our life.

41

———

MRS. CATTANEO

Eleni

I twist the ribbon around my deep purple bouquet and look out over the reception. The wives rented a massive ballroom in a hotel close enough to the church that we all walked over when the ceremony ended, and if you'd asked me to guess what Nicky thought a wedding reception should look like, I would've described exactly this. There's nowhere in this place I can look without being confronted by something that sparkles or bears the exact "eggplant" and "pine forest" that are apparently our colors.

Above every table, something that looks like a baby mobile made out of twinkle lights and strings of crystals hang. On the purple and green tablecloths sit the most ridiculous place settings I've ever seen. The gilt-edged china sports crossed flowers, a dusty green spring of something that looks more like leaves to me but which she said grow around the Acropolis and a sprig of Italian lilac, both also lined in gold. Apparently, they symbolize the joining of our houses. But what really makes me laugh is the silverware. Not for a mafia wedding, the

205

lowly regular knife and fork. No, Nicky ordered in custom flatware with swirled silver-and-gold handles like our rings.

I never would've picked this out for myself in a million years, but honestly? That's perfect.

On the dance floor, Dante swings someone's niece or daughter or cousin, no more than seven years old, around in a circle. Three other little girls stand around him, pulling on his pant legs and begging for their turns. They flocked as soon as my swollen feet grew too tired, and I fled to our glittering sweetheart table. His grin stretches his face, and his purple tie hangs loose around his neck. At the beginning of this summer, I wouldn't have picked him out for myself either.

That Eleni seems so far away now. The good girl who just barely managed to squeeze a couple night classes in between shifts at the diner and making space for herself in the grief surrounding Christos. The one who hurried home, whose world basically stopped at the door to the restaurant, whose sexiest dress was the one she wore to funerals. She found Dante Greek-god handsome but dangerous. Not worth the price of entering his world. She had no idea what it was like to hold a gun, to take a life, to even want someone dead.

I put a hand on my slightly squashed stomach. She also didn't know what it was like to protect someone with her life. Or to love like I do. She was a naïve girl, and I think I'll always miss her a little, but I'm glad I've become the woman who chooses to become Mrs. Cattaneo, even if she doesn't choose anything else about her wedding.

Past the dance floor, next to the towering white wedding cake we haven't yet cut into, a large, round table overflows with laughing, smiling women, nearly all of them over the age of forty. The older wives and nonnas, with Mama smack dab in the middle of them, holding court. Just as soon as we got out of the church—which, she made certain to tell me, was "okay" for Catholics but could've done with a few more spires—she bloomed into a glowing mother-of-the-bride. Maybe even more glowing than I am, between my late night and baby trying to figure out if they hate the lasagna I scarfed for dinner. Now that they can't fight over wedding plans anymore, all the wives seem obsessed with her. The nonnas keep circling her and calling her beautiful, asking if she's sure we're not sisters like they're lecherous old men instead. I haven't been able to pry her away for hours, but watching her smile like this is more than worth it.

My gaze slides back to Dante, now on little girl number two. He said we had time to make our decision, together, but now the wedding's over. What are we waiting for, really? A chance to kill Fyodor, whom he hasn't even gotten close to yet? A sign from God bigger than me suddenly getting pregnant? All this waiting and dragging our feet seems silly. We both know what we want. It's just that neither of us will ask it of the other.

I stand. I'll take the plunge. I'll walk right out onto the dance floor and tell Dante, right here and now, that I want—

Gianna appears like magic and grabs my arm. "Hey! I was just coming to get you."

I blink. "Uh, hey. You look better."

She giggles, and the sleeve of her dress shifts to show a dark hickey one of the many purple-suited groomsmen must've given her. "Hair of the dog."

"You're lucky you don't have a job right now." I shake my head. "Are you getting me for a reason? I was kind of in the middle of something."

"Yes, I definitely am." She glances over her shoulder, her brow furrowed. Then, her face lights. "Yes! It's time for the dance. The circle one?"

I laugh. "Zorbas?"

She nods. "Exactly!"

This has to be Mama's doing. I wouldn't be surprised if she'd been over there teaching the ladies to dance and convincing the band to play her favorite old folk song. The singer taps his mic as Gianna leads me down.

"Alrighty, ladies and gentlemen, it's time for a classic Greek tradition, the Zor-bash!"

Mama scowls, but I can only laugh. Dante grins when I reach him.

"I don't know how to do this!" he says in my ear.

"Follow my lead." I take his hand.

Mama takes my other, and one of the little girls holds onto Dante. Slowly but surely, a circle of people forms, and the band of twenty-something New Yorkers who look like they took this gig to score cigarette money lurches into a version of Mama's favorite song. We blunder into the dance.

Some people stay on the outside of the circle, just clapping. Many of the nonnas, which is good because I don't really want to end my wedding on a broken hip. More of the men than at a Greek wedding. Tony stands nearby, his arms crossed, and I decide to make fun of him when I pass.

The circle drags me closer, stumbling through the kicks and all laughing. I'm two people away. One. I realize Tony's spooky, ice-blue eyes are trained on something specific behind me.

I twist. There, at the edge of the room, stand two men I don't know. That's not surprising, with how many guests Nicky invited. But their drab, ill-fitting suits do stand out. This wedding is a lot of things, but drab, it is not. One of them checks their phone, then nods to the other. The hair on the back of my neck rises. Together, they begin slicing through the crowd.

Tony's hand lands on mine and Dante's. "We have to move. Now."

"What?" Dante blinks, his eyes hazy with the couple whiskeys he's had.

"Now," Tony hisses.

I release Mama, and start to pull Dante away. The dance falters as people start to realize something is happening.

"Excuse me," one of the men bellows over the song.

I'm not fast. Between the dress, the heels, and baby—I spit in my mind—I'm not going anywhere. So I release Dante and shove him toward Tony, then plant myself in the path of the men.

"How can I help you?" I ask.

In unison, they reach into their jacket, withdraw what look like wallets, and flip them open. The bold, blue letters are unmissable.

FBI.

Organized chaos breaks out. The music cuts off on a sour note. Armed capos flock to the nonnas and take their arms one by one, protecting them and giving themselves the plausible deniability of helping an old woman. I watch dozens of hands go to belts where I know guns wait, then shrink back. The rest of the wives start to form up at my sides, Mama included.

"Apologies, miss, but we have a warrant for the arrest of one Dante Federico Cattaneo." The one on the left looks over my shoulder, where I suspect Dante is. "If you'll come in quietly, we won't prosecute the hundreds of weapons charges in this room."

"No!" I shout. "It's my fucking wedding! You can't have him, not tonight."

The other one shrugs past me, and the *click* of handcuffs echoes through the suddenly silent ballroom.

"Apologies," the first says again. "Have a good rest of your night, Mrs. Cattaneo."

42

BACK IN CHARGE

ELENI

I SLAM my hands down on my desk on the second floor of the Staten Island house, the long sleeves of my wedding dress dulling the thud. "What the fuck do you mean, you don't know?"

Armando, the man I've begun considering my capo, loosens his purple tie and shrugs. "Nobody knows who the fuck they are. I've got a couple reports they were at the church. The guard at the door said he never saw them come in. They're feds, obviously, but did you see the names on the badges?"

"No, I fucking didn't, because I was in the process of having my *husband* arrested at my *wedding!*" I suck in a deep breath and run my hands through my hair. I took it down sometime on the ride from the ballroom to here, but a few pins still *plink* onto the floor around my feet.

I'm losing it. The house is a swarm of activity—wives, trying to get everybody fed; capos, trying to figure this out; guests, just trying to figure out how a wedding went so wrong—and they need a goddamn leader. They need me.

No, they need the me who led them for two weeks the last time Dante got taken out of commission. I roll out my shoulders and let ice slide over the welter of panic and rage and *I told you so* burning beneath the lace of my fucking wedding dress.

"Get me Tony," I bark, "a black coffee, my navy suit from the bedroom, and Dante's secondary laptop from his office."

A few of the other men in the room scurry out, leaving me with Armando and a small handful of other guards. I start opening drawers, pulling out things I need. My favorite pistol and a few spare clips. A hair tie, which my heavily processed curls resist. One of the stupid stress balls Gianna kept pushing on me, this one shaped like the Statue of Liberty.

The door opens, and Tony walks in.

"You spotted them before I did," I say immediately. "How long before?"

He shakes his head. "Maybe a minute before they called for the dance. I don't know if they just walked in or what, but I watched them walk over to the wall and lean there. The one on the left, the taller one, was just hanging up a phone call."

I study him for long enough that someone arrives with my suit, and a steaming coffee appears on my desk. His usually perfectly gelled hair is rumpled, and there's a wild look in his eyes. The jacket of his suit is missing, and his sleeves are rolled up to his elbows. I don't think he's lying.

I didn't expect that to be worse.

"Are they real feds?" I sip my coffee, then start pulling my suit pants on under my dress.

He shrugs. "An illegal gun kills you as dead as a legal one."

Bullshit answer, but it means Dante hasn't popped up on any police scanners. Finally, someone runs in with the spare laptop. I boot it up, wish I hadn't left mine at the apartment in the city, and start scanning his hard drive for any programs I left in there.

"Is there anything you know that I don't?" I ask.

"You know about the brigadier?" Tony glances around the room.

There's about eight people in here, not counting the two of us. Eight too many to say the word "rat." I nod.

"Then no." He scowls. "Two fucking days with the bastard, and he didn't give us another word."

No programs. I'm going to need to code something new. Fuck. I shoot the rest of the coffee, wince at the burn, then turn my back to the room. "Unzip me."

I don't know whose fingers find the metal at my back. It should have been Dante's, but instead, he chose not to listen to me about Henry fucking Alcott, and now he's spending our wedding night in jail. The dress sloughs off my body, and I grab the camisole someone brought with my suit and tug it on.

"Armando, I want you on the scanners. Check every frequency. The feds might have their own. Any whisper of where he's going, and you assemble a team." I shrug the jacket on, pull my hair out of the collar. "Dice, contact the ballroom, get any footage they have of the parking lot. I want to know what car they took him in, and I want that found. Tony, chase what we learned from the brigadier." I stare out the dark window ahead of me. "By whatever means necessary."

"*Zouzouni?*"

I whip around to see Mama in the doorway, flanked by burly capos. Her mother-of-the-bride dress is wrinkled, her sweater hangs off one shoulder like she forgot about it, and her face is pale with worry.

"Mama." I step around the desk. "Now isn't a great time. Please, go back downsta—"

Worry transforms into anger in a split second. "No."

"What?"

"No." She crosses her arms. "I will not let you do this."

The thick layer of ice over my feelings makes me scowl. "Everybody else, out. Stand by the door if you fucking have to but close it behind you.'

Capos file out of the room. In the corner of my eye, Tony shoots me a look, but I ignore him to stare at Mama. The door shuts.

"I'm an adult," I say. "A married woman. You don't get to let me do things."

She shakes her head slowly. "I thought you were going to school, *zouzouni*."

"I am!" I throw my hands in the air. "But sometimes, the Saints need me."

"Dante needs you." She takes a step closer. "Forget this. Come downstairs and worry with the rest of us. Leave the business to people who know it."

"I know it," I reply. "I ran this organization for weeks. I've never really left it. People listen to me."

She quivers, and tears trail down her cheeks for what must be the hundredth time today. "Please. I—we lost Christos to this life. We lost Baba. Do not make me lose you."

Dimly, I'm aware that the person I was this morning would've been devastated by those tears, by that statement.

"I don't have a choice," I say. "You're right, Dante needs me. Like this."

She takes another step forward, closing the distance between us, and reaches up. For a moment, I think she's going to stroke my hair, like when I was a little girl with a fever. I don't know what that will do to the ice in my chest.

Something in my curls loosens, and she withdraws her hand with the red flower sitting in her palm. I completely forgot about that.

"This was for you to borrow," she says quietly. "I think I will take it back now."

Mama turns and walks out. A few capos—thankfully, less the ones I assigned tasks so I don't have to start breaking kneecaps—peer into the open doorway.

"You're guards, aren't you?" I ask sharply. "Get in here and fucking guard."

I return to the desk I've only really used as the Queen of the Saints and begin coding a program to access the local FBI database.

SOMEWHERE IN NEW YORK

Dante

MY WRISTS BURN from twisting them against the zip cuffs, my ankles chafe from the same treatment around the legs of the chair, my shoulders ache from how far my arms have been pulled back, my faces throbs from how many times these goddamn bruisers have hit me, but all I can think about is El.

I should be home in bed with her right now, fighting with whatever fiddly little fixtures they put on her wedding dress. She should be screaming my name. I should be screaming hers.

Instead, I'm sitting in a musty-ass basement, bound to a metal chair under one flickering light like these assholes got their set-up right out of an '80s mafia movie. I spit blood on the concrete floor and look up at the man who "arrested" me in the middle of my goddamn wedding.

"So tell me," I say, "how do you go from Coppola to the Russians?"

That, of course, earns me another punch to the face. I grit my teeth and take it.

"Cuteness isn't going to get you far," Jace growls. "I'm here to get answers, and I'm happy to take them back with a pound of flesh."

"I hope a pound of flesh is answer enough, cause it's all you're getting," I reply.

"You cocky son of a bitch." He pulls back for another hit.

"Hold." The thick, heavily accented voice echoes from a corner of this fucking room too dark for me to see into yet.

I twist as much as I can in my bounds anyway, ignoring the way my skin screams. "We got an audience? You should've let me know, I could've performed better."

Jace snarls. Out of the shadows steps a muscle bound man in a dove gray suit that fits him with the unmistakable precision of custom work. He's skipped a tie, leaving his white shirt open to show a bed of silvery chest hair that matches the coif on his head. His jaw makes him look like a bruiser, but the tip of one highly decorative star peeking out through the chest hair indicates a twin on his other shoulder and a highly ranked criminal.

I've never seen his face before, but I have a sense I already know who I'm talking to.

"Fyodor," I say. "Or do you prefer Raskolnikov?"

He chuckles, low and dangerous. "I like a cocky man."

I grin. "Then you're going to be thrilled with me."

"They are much more fun to break." Fyodor nods to Jace.

Before I can brace for the impact, Jace slams his fist into my gut, and I fold. My stomach riots. I gasp in a breath and straighten as quickly as I'm able.

"What's the point?" I hiss. "Aren't your men powerful enough to just take the city by force?"

Fyodor scoffs. "Of course they are. But you and I both know any boss worth his salt misses the streets when he leaves them."

So I can't goad him into violence by taunting his abilities. Maybe by taunting him in general. I need a new tactic.

"I'm, what, a playmate for you?" I smirk. "You know, I got married tonight, so that should've told you my—"

Jace smashes a metal baton into my knee, and I choke down a yell.

Someone grabs my hair and yanks my head back up. I stare into Fyodor's nearly white-gray eyes.

"I do know this," he says. "Why do you think I took you tonight? You Italians always need a reminder that you're not nearly as invincible as you seem to believe."

"Arresting me is a shitty power play," I reply. "I don't even think Jace has his badge anymore."

"Ha! You think we need badges?" Fyodor's smile is vicious. "Goes to show how small your mind is."

The pain is starting to blot out my higher-thinking skills. I know one thing for certain: I'm not going to break down here. I hope to hell I'm not going to die. A quick check reveals my wedding ring still nestled on my finger, and posing as two fucking feds, the Russians couldn't exactly put a dent in my men. Or El. So she'll have already remembered that, and they'll be on their way to me just as soon as they can. I start rubbing one of the jagged edges of one of the stones against the plastic of the cuffs. All I need to do is keep my mouth shut long enough to survive.

That's never been my way. The word "rat" keeps circling in my head. If anyone knows who it is, it's Fyodor. And I can't go home without making sure this can't happen again.

"Fine. Help out a moron then." I look up at him, trying to seem tired. "What the hell did I miss?"

Fyodor laughs again. "Too easy, Italian. I know you are not done so early." He shakes his head. "But equally I know you're never leaving this basement alive, and there wasn't shit you could do anyway. Fine, then. Perform for me."

Half a dozen blows with the baton land in rapid succession. My shoulder, my knee again, my ribs. I can feel bones cracking, taste nothing but blood. All I have down here is my pride.

And the certainty El is coming. So I yell for Fyodor, feeling as low as a fucking snake when he smiles with sick pleasure.

"Good, good."

Jace stops.

"You are not so polite to your pets," Fyodor says. "Young Henry was quite happy for a kinder master."

Fucking Henry Alcott. El warned me, and I ignored her. Hell, Tony warned me. I never should've gotten in bed with him. And now, he's ruined my goddamn wedding.

Oh, I'm going to destroy him when I get out of here.

"Why just take me, then?" I wheeze. "Henry hates us all."

"That he does." Fyodor inclines his head to me like he's a teacher, and I'm his pupil. "But young Henry needs to learn patience. And I only need you. Who else? Should I take your blushing bride, before the whole city remembers they want her blood to run in the streets for her crimes? Your half-dead caporegime, still sick with grief over his baby brother?" He laughs. "No, your Saints will destroy themselves prettily without you."

My blood burns. "Keep them out of your fucking mouth."

Fyodor just laughs and gestures to Jace, who lets loose again.

He must've paid Henry to turn. Whatever the fuck else that scumsucker is, he knows Tony's nonna, his nonna, is going to get caught up in this. Jace would've flipped for a candy bar, but Henry doesn't want that.

"You're going to have to kill me," I say.

"That can be arranged," Fyodor replies.

4 4

———

TIES THAT BIND

Eleni

I sit in the passenger seat of a black, bulletproof sedan, watching the blinking dot of the tracker on my phone. "Left here."

Tony turns smoothly. The engine is nearly silent, which seems almost pointless in the noisy, New York City night, but I'm not giving up any advantage here. It took me embarrassingly long to remember the tracker—or, more accurately, to hope the feds hadn't bothered to take it off him. I was halfway through hacking the city's FBI base when I looked down at my own hand and the rings caught the light.

"And…that's the last precinct turnoff I know of," Mikey says from the back seat, where he's sliding together piece after piece of a sniper rifle, just in case. "Bronx cops don't bother with spots this far out."

"Me either," Tony says. "Maybe they took him to one of those fucking black sites."

Distantly, I note a chill of worry would touch me at those words, if I weren't already frozen.

"You're sure you don't remember the names on any of the badges?" I ask. "Turn right."

219

He turns. "One of 'em started with a 'J.' Nothing more."

"Fine." I sigh.

The car continues cutting through the night. We passed the way to the FBI Headquarters ages ago. Mikey has checked off each precinct as we skip it. The crowds don't taper off as we nearly drive out of the city, just the working streetlights. Maybe they took Dante to a black site. Or maybe we're not the only people in the fucking world with dirty feds. Hell, maybe someone bought ours. If there's one thing I've learned these last few months, it's that someone who will turn once will always turn twice. That's why I was wiping out Coppola men instead of sparing them. Their word wouldn't mean shit to me.

I check the bullets in the pistol at my waist and think about the private plane, gassed up and ready to go, at the airstrip north of the city. A suitcase sits in the hold with enough cash to get me out. Not just me. Not even just with Baby—I spit in my mind—but Mama and Gianna too. We'll be set for life. Just before I turned on the tracker, I told every Saint to call his family and set them up just like that.

Wait for the phone. Be ready to run.

The whole world feels like it's on tenterhooks, waiting for the outcome. Will the Saints win? Or will they abandon New York City to the dogs?

If Dante were here, he'd tell me to get on the plane now. Fuck the mission, the men have it. But if he were in my shoes, he wouldn't dream of leaving before he had me back. I'm fucking tired of the double standards. I'll rescue him or see his body.

Then, I'll leave. For him. For Baby.

At least if he's in custody, the papers we signed just hours earlier mean we won't be forced to testify against each other.

My phone beeps softly, alerting me that we're close. Half-collapsed or mostly dark buildings stick out between brightly lit ones that look almost as bad. The streets still crowd with people.

"Tony," I say.

He glances at me. "I think you're supposed to have cold feet before the wedding."

"Fuck off," I reply automatically.

He waves a hand for me to continue.

"If he's dead, the Saints are yours," I say.

Tony raises an eyebrow.

"Dead," I repeat, the word landing hollowly on my chest, "dying, in federal custody. Any of those, I have to run."

"I should already be looking at your back," he mutters.

I'd like to say I responded with anger, but that would be a lie. Every inch of my skin is cold, every movement of my body certain, as I slide my gun from my holster, cock it, and place it against his temple.

"Say it again."

"I'll say it." Mikey puts a hand on my wrist. "You have to relax."

I don't look away from Tony. My fingers don't shake.

"I'm giving you everything you want," I say. "Take it without bitching."

"I told you you were cut out for this life," Tony mutters.

That's as much of an apology as I'm going to get from him. I remove the gun from his temple and slide it back away.

"Last turn," I say. "Park here, and we'll walk."

Tony obeys. "Looks like an apartment block. No lights. Gotta be empty."

"Vests." Mikey hands forward two bulletproof vests.

I pull off my suit jacket, slip the vest on under it, then adjust the straps around the stomach aggressively. I owe Dante a rescue, but I also owe Baby a fair chance at life.

Tony, already wearing his, adjusts my shoulder straps. "I don't give a fuck, but Seb would."

"Maybe tomorrow, that'll mean something." I pull my jacket back on and button it. Anything I can put between Baby and the world.

He leans back. "You're really gonna make me do this? Hold your ass while you die, knowing I never really liked you but it's gonna kill Dante if the Russians haven't already?"

I'm done. I meet Tony's ice gaze. "Yes. Tonight. Tomorrow night. Forever, if I damn well please. You've known him for longer, fine. You've got history, seniority, whatever the fuck you want. But he's my fucking husband"—I point to the twin rings on my finger—"and that means I'm not leaving him to die. I'm not taking a single chance. And there's nobody on this team who will fight harder than me to get him back."

Tony holds my gaze for a long moment, then looks away. "Yeah, that's what I'm afraid of."

Before I can reply to that, Mikey's phone rings. He answers immediately.

"Hey, Leo."

Leo is part of the advance team, the guys who weren't running around doing shit and we already set to go. I crane my head to see if I can hear through Mikey's phone speakers.

Mikey frowns. "Wait, you're—what the fuck, man?"

At the apartment block, something flashes. A shot rings out.

I throw myself out of the car.

45

HESITATION

Eleni

Tony hits the ground running in front of me, already yanking his gun out of his holster. Mikey fumbles with the door a second, but he's out immediately after that, the carefully laid plan of the sniper rifle abandoned behind him. I slam down the pavement, thankful I abandoned my usual heels in favor of a pair of sneakers Gianna offered me silently before we left. Different windows of the apartment block light in bright bursts. Muzzle flashes, I know. The attendant *pop* of the gunfire follows on their heels, like thunder after lighting. People scatter out of our way. I grip my gun at my side. No sweat makes it slip. The leather warms in my palm as I run through scenarios.

If they're keeping Dante at the top, we'll have to fight our way up. But that also means they're vulnerable to attacks from above, if we had the time to set that up. I told someone to call in all the allies we have, but that doesn't make a difference. It's not like Cal or the triads are about to loan us a helicopter on short notice.

If they're keeping him in the middle, that's the real bitch. We would have to search every floor of the towering apartment building.

My heart hammers, but my breathing is smooth, so I try to count the floor as I run up. Ten, fifteen, twenty-five.

What the hell am I doing? We've been fighting the Russians for months now, and they're smart, but everybody relies on familiar tactics. They kept me in the basement. Dante will be as low as they can get him.

"When we get inside," I call, "head—"

Someone swings out of an alley, and I whip around, bringing my gun up to shoulder height. Line up the shot. Know you want to take that life. I squeeze one eye shut and look at the armed target in front of me.

Who puts up his hands. "Should've known the Queen of Saints would be here, I s'pose."

The Irish brogue reaches my ears. The moon shines on dark red hair.

"Cal." I lower my gun. "Shouldn't have jumped out at me like that."

"Apologies, lass." He bows.

More gunfire cuts through the night. I whirl and keep running. Luckily, Cal keeps up.

"Went to the trouble of dialing old Wing," he says. "They should be circling in from the north."

I nod sharply, my gut churning. I almost shot him. I have to find the line between fast enough to save Dante and too fast to think. Another second, and we'd have lost an important ally.

"Just you?" Tony asks.

"Ah, I sent my lads on a pincer, since you'd arrive fastest south." Cal shoots me a wink. "Apologies for the lack of warning, but the avenging angel look does suit you."

I make a face. I can't imagine where it lands between smile and snarl. Whatever it is, it makes Cal look quickly away.

"No sign of feds," he says.

"Gee, you think?" Tony snaps. "I thought they loved abandoned housing projects. We're off the fucking map here."

We skid to a stop at the arched, rickety-looking entrance to the building.

"Down," I say. "Head down. They're going to be in the lowest basement."

Tony looks at me for a second, like he's trying to decide if I'm right. *Think, Eleni, don't just act.* I don't scream at him.

He turns into the building without a word. Hopefully, he—

Gunshots ring out, far closer now. A bullet lodges in the cracked wood next to my head. I flatten myself against an exterior wall. Someone yells something in Russian.

Six bullets in the chamber. Inhale. Know you want to take this life.

I lean out, spot a Russian behind a fallen row of mail cubbies, and fire. He spins away, his shoulder spouting blood.

"No time to waste!" I call as I duck back. "Move when you see an opening."

On the opposite side of the entrance, Mikey nods at me, then darts inside. There's a spray of gunfire, but no pain noises. He's inside. Headed down, hopefully.

Five bullets. I lean back out and hit the jackpot. Two Russians, one of which is supporting his bleeding friend. I pull the trigger twice, smoothly. Both of them fall.

"My queen." Cal flips a teasing salute at me and starts to saunter inside.

The first Russian I shot looms back over the mail cubbies.

"Cal!" I yell.

He starts to turn, but it's too late. The Russian shoots him in the hip, and he topples. I plug the bastard in the middle of the fucking forehead. This time, he's not getting back up. Nobody else emerges into the entrance, so Tony darts out for Cal. I keep my gun—two bullets in the chamber—raised, waiting. After a moment, he starts to help Cal stand. Not dead, but they can't move fast. I should move in.

Think, El, don't just act!

If I leave them behind, I lose two of the best fighters I could have at my back. Cal's a demon, and Tony is Dante's right hand for a reason. But if I help them, what's the best case? We dump Cal outside, and Tony and I move on? I'll lose precious seconds of potentially saving Dante.

Someone moves in my peripheral vision. Think, don't act. I glance out of the corner of my eye.

Outside the building, approaching along the wall, is Henry fucking Alcott. I'd recognize that slick smile anywhere. He has a gun drawn—not his service weapon—but held low at his side. He thinks he's sneaking up on me.

Cal groans. Thinking is no longer the order of the day.

Like lightning, I whip around, take aim, and fire. Henry stumbles as I hit him in the stomach, smears blood along the rough concrete wall. I advance on him. One bullet left. He looks up at me, and I don't know how I thought he ever looked like Seb.

I fire my last bullet directly into his brain. Hesitation is dead, and so is Henry Alcott.

Tony whistles for me to catch up. Without a second to waste, I turn and run into the building.

4 6

WEDDING NIGHT

Dante

Jace is glaring at me sullenly from the other side of the room they're keeping me in when the first gunshots ring out.

"What the fuck?" he says.

I grin. El's here. Hopefully with the cavalry in tow. I scrape the stone in my ring over the plastic faster and faster. I'm almost through, and now, I have nothing to lose in Jace seeing me.

"Wait, what the fuck are you doing?" He leaps to his feet.

Out of time. Better hope I sawed enough. I tense my arms and yank.

One of the cuffs snaps just as Jace throws himself at me, his baton raised for another strike. Idiot. I use the momentum of the cuffs breaking to swing my right fist forward, directly into his cheek. The blow knocks him off balance just enough that I can drive my elbow into the meat of his bicep—not impressive-looking, but it makes him whimper—and that exposes his right side. Where the fucking moron still has his service weapon holstered. I snatch it out and fire two shots point-blank into his chest.

Before he even hits the floor, I'm bending over him as much as I can with my ankles still bound to this fucking chair and fumbling through his pockets. Ah! On his waistband, he has exactly what I need: a pocket knife. With what looks like a mother-of-pearl handle, but at least he's a dead douchebag. I slit the plastic holding my legs in place and jump to my feet. Somebody will be coming for me soon, and I'm praying it's Fyodor. I tuck myself against the wall, right where the door will hide me while it opens, and wait.

One heartbeat passes. Two. I check Jace's gun over quickly. Semi-auto, two bullets used. He probably has more magazines, if I need to fight my way out. Footsteps pound toward me. I brace.

The door opens, and I see a flash of dove gray fabric in the crack. Perfect.

I slam the door back, and whoever was opening it grunts as it hopefully gives them a hell of a concussion. Then, I jump forward and yank the door open again. Element of surprise.

Gun smoke makes the hallway hazy, but I can see Fyodor and two guards clearly. My body moves automatically. Arms up, first goon sighted, bullet between the eyes. He topples. Again, and the second guard falls like clockwork.

"Italian bastard!" Fyodor bellows.

I should've known Russians wouldn't have the polish for an out-and-out gunfight. The leader of the organization that's been torturing me for months throws himself at me like a fucking linebacker, and we hit the ground in a pile. I bite back a scream as he lands on my probably broken ribs. Jace's gun scatters away. Fuck!

Fyodor doesn't give me enough space to reach for it. He keeps me pressed to the floor, his body barely an inch from mine, and begins pummeling me. My fists slam into his ribs, but the baton blow to my shoulder weakens the hit.

Through the haze of blood and pain, I note the rings tattooed on his knuckles. They probably mean a bunch of different shit, but there's only one thing about them I need to know. He did a stint in a Russian prison, and probably a long one. Which means he knows how to scrap with the best of them.

I can fight dirty if he wants me to.

The next time one of his hits brings him close to my face, I lunge up, capture a mouthful of ear, and bite down. Blood spurts, hot and coppery, into my mouth. Fyodor howls. I spit the chunk of his flesh away and use the brief gap that earned me to hook my leg around his, brace an elbow on the floor, and roll us over. Just a little closer to Jace's gun. Once Fyodor's back hits the floor, I start to stand and race for the deadly weapon.

He whips out a straight knife from a holster I didn't see on his belt and stabs it through the hand I'm using to push myself up, trapping me against a small crack in the cement floor that catches the blade.

"Fuck!"

He laughs, the side of his head covered in blood. "Looking for this?"

Fyodor pulls another gun from his belt.

I yank against the knife pinning me to the floor, but that only makes pain spread like fire up my arm. Leisurely, he cocks the gun.

Holy shit. I've lost.

El, if you can hear me, I love you, I think out into the universe. *I always loved you. Take Baby and live a beautiful life for me.*

The last thing I expect is for Fyodor to slide out from underneath me and saunter back to the door. My heart leaps into my throat. I fucking missed something. I grab the knife with my other hand and pull as hard as I can. The blade slips free a second after a gunshot rings out.

My mind goes white. I scramble for Jace's gun, whip around, and riddle Fyodor's body with bullets until the pistol clicks. Empty. I throw the husk of the weapon down and scramble out into the hall, over the dead Russian.

There, flat on her back in the hazy hallway, lays El.

"No, no, no," someone moans.

I race to her side. I can barely see. There's blood everywhere. I don't know what's hers or mine or any of the dead Russians in the hallway. I stroke her cheek, and she doesn't respond.

Not her. Anyone but her. If they've killed her, and Fyodor is already dead, I won't be able to stop until I've brought the whole fucking FBI down. My eyes slide shut, and I gather her to my chest. She's still warm and pliant.

Footsteps pound toward me. Let them kill me now. Who gives a fuck?

"Dante," Tony says.

I open my eyes and look up at him. He's bloody but walking.

"They got her," I whisper.

"Fuck." Tony drops to his knees next to me, knocks my arms away, and rips open El's jacket, presumably to start doing the first aid I hadn't even thought of yet.

The most beautiful thing I've ever seen stares back at me. A navy-blue bulletproof vest with a bronze shell casing lodged visibly in its surface.

El coughs, and her beautiful blue eyes flicker open. "Dante?"

A wild smile splits my face. "Thank God."

I crush her back to my chest, despite how much it hurts me, and she holds me back.

"Not how I…pictured it," she says.

"What?" I ask.

She laughs weakly. "Our wedding night."

Hot tears slip down my cheeks. I press kisses to her hair and promise that I love her. But over the top of her head, I meet Tony's eyes. He looks exhausted like he didn't a minute ago, and I think he already knows what I'm going to say. Somehow, that makes it harder.

"I'm fucking done," I say. "I can't do this anymore."

Tony closes his eyes.

4 7

ENOUGH TIME

ELENI

I CLOSE my eyes on the floor in Dante's arms and open them again somewhere warm and tan and lonely. Distantly, I can hear voices. My stomach aches.

My stomach! I shoot up, yank up the "I Heart NYC" shirt covering my abdomen for some reason, and probe the skin there. I was shot. Someone—Fyodor, judging by how much nicer his suit was—shot me in the stomach, like he knew exactly who I was. But there's no gaping bullet hole, not even a careful line of black stitches.

Because I wore the stupid bulletproof vest, I've got a welt, a bruise so dark it's almost black, and a hell of a headache from the bullet knocking me on my ass, and nothing more.

The voices raise slightly, and a door I hadn't noticed yet opens. Dante steps in wearing a matching T-shirt with his arm in a sling. Behind him, Dr. Domino frowns.

"You're up," Dante says breathlessly.

Everything hits me at once. He's here. I'm here. We're both alive. And I don't think he'd be looking at me with that sunrise light in his

231

eyes if anything happened to Baby—though I spit in my head auto-matically. He takes a step, clearly about to charge across the room to me.

Dr. Domino clears his throat. "I would advise both of my patients to take it easy, for the sake of my third."

Dante's jaw works. "You're a good doc, Domino, but I'm going to need you to butt out this time."

I laugh. Dante's voice is beautiful.

"Fine!" Dr. Domino throws his hands up. "See what I care. You're getting on a fucking plane, anyway." He yanks a few orange prescription bottles out of the pocket of his leather duster. "Take these if you don't want to die of infection."

He slams them down on top of the mini-fridge next to the door and storms out.

Dante doesn't wait a second before racing to join me in bed. Still, I notice the way his left leg drags behind him a little. And the sling—

"You're hurt," I say.

"I've had worse." He grins and lays down on the thin mattress next to me. "And anyway, I feel a hell of a lot better looking at you."

I purse my lips despite the euphoria racing through my veins. "Nope. Tell me the truth, or I'll run away."

He sighs, but even his sigh has the texture of a laugh. "Of course you will. Fyodor—Artyom, according to his internal records—beat the shit out of me. And so did Jace, that other fed. I've got a couple stab wounds, a metric fuckton of bruises, and only a few fractures."

I wince and run my fingers over the purple skin of his shoulder. "Seems bruises are something we have in common."

Dante grunts. "Ah, actually, one of those fractures would be my collarbone. Watch the pressure."

"Sorry!" I jerk my hand back. "They work quickly."

He nods. "But luckily, so do we."

"Do we?" I ask, staring up into his night-black eyes and hoping he'll read the real question underneath.

"If you're asking about the business, they're all dead." He brushes a few hairs back from my face with his undamaged hand. "Fyodor,

Henry. Apparently, you killed him. A few Russians got out, but Tony's leading a cleanup crew."

I killed a federal agent. My stomach turns.

"And if I'm not asking about the business?" My voice shakes slightly.

"Then you're all right except for a concussion and that bruise we have in common." He smiles softly. "Baby seems all right too."

A tear slips down my cheek. "What do we do now?"

"We get on the plane you had waiting." He kisses the tear away. "And we go to Greece with Mama and Gianna. After that, you tell me, El. Are we vacationing or making a life for ourselves?" His eyes are dark and earnest. "I know what I want."

I open and close my mouth a few times. All the ice I built up around myself is already gone. It was too fragile this time, threatening to crack every time I thought about Baby. And without it, without all the distractions and threats and pressure, the answer is obvious. Maybe it always has been.

"We're building a life," I whisper. "If you're sure you can give this up."

Dante laughs. "Sure? El, I can't wait. I love you, and loving you made me someone completely different. Someone who can't sit around plotting in my little office, satisfied with the violence and power plays of the life I was raised to lead. Nothing matters more to me than you and"—he smooths his hand over my distended stomach, carefully avoiding the welt—"Baby. I can't be the boss they need while loving you, and I don't want to stop that."

Something warm and soft blooms in my chest. He really is a different man than the one I met. The Dante who threw fifty thousand dollars at me to get me out of his auction would never do this.

"And I can't be the boss they need and the woman you love." I put my hand over his. "Or the mother they need. Maybe a mother at all. And they deserve better than that. Better than we had."

"So that's it." He kisses me on each of my cheeks. "We're done. I'll hand the reins to Tony, and we'll live our little dream life."

"Not so little," I say. "I'm still going to school."

He nods seriously. "I wouldn't dream of anything else."

"And I don't really think parenthood's going to be little." I smile.

"You may be more right about that than I'd hope." He grins ruefully.

I trace the lines of his hand, his wedding ring. "So…what's with the T-shirts?"

Dante falls back, laughing wildly. "We were covered in blood, and we're in a crappy little motel outside the city, maybe twenty minutes from the airstrip. The gift shop was all I had."

I laugh with him. "I spent all this time picking out lingerie, and now I'm spending my wedding night with no bra, no underwear, in a tourist T-shirt!"

"Don't worry, I saw the lingerie. I liked it." He waggles his eyebrows. "I think we can take it carry-on."

I swat him. "Not if Mama's there."

"Fine, we'll buy new." He shakes his head, and his laughter starts to die down.

"How long until we have to get on the plane anyway?" I ask quietly.

Dante smiles just a little wickedly. "Enough time for a wedding night, if you still want one with an ex-mafia boss."

"I don't," I say.

His mouth falls open.

"I want one with Dante Cattaneo, my husband." And I kiss him.

48

'TIL DEATH DO US PART

ELENI

DANTE SURGES up into my mouth, then grunts in pain. I pull back immediately.

"And what if your husband just got the shit kicked out of him?" He smiles sheepishly and gestures to the sling on his arm.

Even when he was shot, he didn't ask for anything. He really is a different man now.

"Doesn't change a thing." I climb slowly on top of him. My side aches, and my head spins a little. I brace my arms on either side of his head and lean down to kiss him again.

His mouth slots perfectly into mine. I know the taste of his lips, the half-gasp that precedes his cock stiffening underneath me, the flutter of his fingers over my bruise. I've spent so much time thinking about how well Dante knows me that I never even realized how well I know him. My hips begin moving against him of their own accord in a slow, undulating rhythm.

He groans against my lips.

"Fuck these shirts." I try to yank his shirt over his head, but the sleeve gets caught on his sling, and I begin laughing.

"What?" He runs his hands along my sides, rucking up the stupid T-shirt.

"This is…perfect." I shake my head. "For us."

His laughter joins mine. "I guess severely injured sex undercover in a motel is kind of par for the course these last few months."

"And I wouldn't have it any other way."

Carefully, we remove as much of his shirt as we can, leaving the one sleeve around his bicep. I press my mouth to his chest, avoiding the bruises but not the now-pale scar from when Luca Lombardi shot him. The coils of dark hair on his skin scrape my cheeks deliciously. He winds his good hand into my hair and just holds on, not pushing me any which way. I'm his anchor in a storm of sensation. I circle my tongue against one of his nipples, coaxing another groan from his lips, then drag it down to the hem of his equally NYC-branded sweatpants.

I gasp. Bending like that compresses the skin around my welt with a burst of pain, and not the sort that makes me wetter. Dante grabs my chin and forces me to look at him.

"Tonight, we're both going to be gentle with ourselves," he says.

There's only the barest hint of iron command in his voice. He's not taking charge, just telling me my pain matters to him as much as his does to me. The quiet acknowledgment of how far we've come shivers through my body.

"I love you." I smile and kiss back up his chest.

"I love you," he groans, "Mrs. Cattaneo."

The name feels like fireworks across my skin. I pull my own T-shirt off and toss it aside. Dante stares at me like I'm a work of art, and I soak it in. Then, he glides his bandaged hand up my ribs—because his other is in the sling, and he can't get it high enough—and palms one of my breasts.

I arch, rolling my hips against him. He matches my thrust, setting a rhythm that's slow like a crashing wave, and toys with me at the same pace. The bandage adds a unique friction, damages his dexterity, but he's my Dante. My husband. His every touch is electric.

He tries to switch to my other breast, winces again at some injury I haven't found yet, and the answer is immediately obvious. I cup the flesh he can't reach, twirl my own nipple. His mouth falls slightly slack. We all match the rhythm of our hips, and it feels like I'm surrounded by him even as he lays flat on the bed. I moan his name, soft and pleading.

"Again." His voice is rough.

"Dante," I moan. "Mr. Cattaneo."

He groans and pinches my nipple. The pain sparks, but I don't need it tonight. I hurt in enough places. So, I think, does he.

On the next roll, one of my hips locks a little, and the bruise burns. Of course it spreads all the way down there. I scowl.

Dante stops immediately. "El?"

I shake my head. "I'm all right, it's just—"

"You can't stay on top." He glances at his injured arms in turn. "And neither can I."

I smile ruefully. "Maybe we've lost our wedding night after all."

"Never." Real anger crosses Dante's face. "I'm not letting them take another goddamn second from us."

He is a different man, but so much the same. I don't want him to ever lose that protective rage. Nothing else makes me feel so safe.

I look him over, then me, and inspiration strikes. I climb off, my hip aching, and shimmy out of my sweatpants. I barely notice I'm naked until I reach for his pants, and he stops me with a bandaged hand on my wrist.

"Let me admire my bride."

I roll my eyes but turn slowly. There's no shame left between us, no part of me he doesn't know as well as I do. And I know what I look like. The soft pouch of my ever-growing stomach, the swell of my hips and my breasts. In not hiding myself from him, I forgot to hide from myself.

Finally satisfied, he nods. I pull his pants off to reveal a brace on one of his knees, but thankfully, it's on the same side as his injured arm, the same side as my welt. My plan will still work.

With gentle hands and kisses, I turn him onto his left side. Then, I climb back on the bed with him, facing the same way, and nestle into the spoon of his body. We fit together like puzzle pieces. His cock is painfully hard against my lower back, and the rest of him burns like a flame.

"So smart," he breathes in my ear. "What would I do without you?"

He wraps his arm, which is still in a sling, around my ribcage and cups one of my breasts as I position his cock between my legs.

"Hurt yourself, probably," I reply with a smile.

"I don't even want to imagine." He thrusts into me, slow and sweet.

His bruised fingers dance over my pebbled skin. I reach back and grab his muscled ass, allowing only a few centimeters of movement. Our chests rise and fall in unison, mine filling the space his vacates. We fuck to that same timeless rhythm, and I start to think this might go on forever. That I've reached the absolute apex of my happiness, ascended, and this will be the rest of my days. I wouldn't mind one bit.

Then, Dante grazes his hand over my stomach, and I remember how much more joy we have coming. Not just a beautiful baby, but a life with them, cleaning up and chasing after and making more. I pull him even closer, piston my hips back. I want this to end, now, because tomorrow is even more beautiful. For the first time in a long time.

I come with his name on my lips, and he follows me a second later.

Tinny music starts blaring from somewhere, and I grope the bed wildly for it. Together, we locate a burner phone singing a shitty little alarm labeled "Get to the plane now." Dante falls back onto the bed with a groan.

"Let's miss this one," he says. "We can always catch up."

I slide off him, sore, wet, and sated. "No way. I'm getting a start on my new—*our* new life." I hold out a hand and smile.

Dante never could refuse me anything.

49

TWO AND A HALF YEARS LATER

Eleni

"Fuck you too!" I yell at a taxi driver leaning on his horn in the center of Athens, yanking my handlebars so I just barely avoid slamming into his hood.

This is what I get for taking a class that gets out at two. But this is the only time Professor Vasiliatos offers his thesis review. Tasia's going to be furious.

Still, by the time I make it far enough out of the city center to smell the ocean breeze, a little of my irritation has burned off. The start of a new semester is always like this. I always decide I never should've taken these classes or this major or decided for the umpteenth time that the feeling of freedom on a bike is more important to me than the ease of a driver. And as soon as I get used to the routine, it'll feel as easy as breathing.

Just like wheeling my bike up to the whitewashed house with the cobalt shutters towering over the restaurant—Gregorio's, for Baba. I chain it to the post out back and dart inside.

Warm cooking smells overwhelm me, along with the clatter of a full kitchen. I duck under a white-coated arm and leap over one of the new hires, crouched on the floor trying to find something. At the center of the chaos stands Mama, directing it like a symphony. No sign of Tasia, but that doesn't mean anything. Ismene, our hostess, sometimes takes her out front because she's "good for business."

"Mama!" I call.

She looks up and smiles, but she doesn't move away from whatever she's stirring on her industrial stove. A class that gets out at two means I arrive in the middle of the lunch rush, too.

"Where's Tasia?" I ask.

"Upstairs," Mama replies. "And I haven't seen Dante yet."

I grimace and race upstairs. Late, late, late.

Dante's voice floats down the stairs before I even reach the top. "Oh, you're not tired? Well, what about…this!"

High, sweet giggles chase his words. I reach the top of the stairs and stop. In the middle of the rug that covers the tile floor, Dante holds two-year-old Anastasia in a mock version of a headlock. She squirms, laughing.

"Come on, Tasia, you're Greek!" he goads. "Your ancestors invented wrestling."

Tasia should be down for her nap by now, so Dante can go back to work, but she won't go down without me here. Still, my heart feels like it's about to burst. She has his dark curls, and when she twists her head back to look at me, she has the same blue eyes as Mama and I. My beautiful baby girl.

"Mama!" she shrieks, throwing herself against Dante's hold.

He releases her with a smile, and she pelts across the floor to throw herself at my legs. I stroke her hair for a second. Everything is sunny, and warm, and no one has pointed a gun at us in over two years.

Tasia has my patience, though, so she begins trying to climb my legs. I scoop her up.

"Have you been giving your papa trouble?" I ask.

She shakes her head, giggling.

With a snort, Dante begins gathering up her toys.

"So when I take you for your nap, you're going to go down nice and easy?" I say coaxingly.

Tasia screws up her face but nods. "Like I promised."

"Good girl." I kiss her on the forehead and start toward her room. On the way, I pause next to Dante. "We're still on for tonight, right?"

He grins. "Wouldn't miss it. I just have a few hours of work to do."

My already bursting heart fills a little more when I remember that he means keeping the books for the restaurant, and that nobody is going to point a gun at him, either.

IN OUR OWN KITCHEN, Mama sits at the table that evening. "No, Demi, the *dill*. How many times do I have to tell you?"

I lean against the counter, fixing my earrings in a mirror I put in the kitchen for just this reason. "Mama, be nice."

"I will be nice when she listens." Mama crosses her arms. "You want my *engoni* eating bad food?"

I mouth "sorry" to Demi, the private chef we hired for our own meals last year, when Mama started to slow down a little. Demi, who's both classically trained and a surprisingly good sport, just shrugs.

Tasia claps in her booster seat. "Tanks, Yia-Yia!"

"That's right, I look out for you," Mama says to her.

Which is a funny way to say "spoil her endlessly," but I can't be mad. Tasia deserves it. I adjust the multi-tonal blue dress Gianna brought back from her last trip to Italy. She stayed with us for a while, but apparently, in Europe, the sedentary life just isn't good enough for her. The dress brings out my eyes and the stone in my engagement ring. Dante will love it, and it's perfect for the restaurant he picked.

I smile at myself in the mirror. No new scars collect on my skin, but I've got the first signs of wrinkles, and a couple gray hairs. Tasia is a handful. Every time I find a new one, Dante kisses it and tells me I'm just catching up. He really is perfect.

"How do I look?" I ask Mama and Tasia both.

"Pity!" Tasia declares.

Mama purses her lips. "That neckline, *zouzouni*...."

I laugh. Mama will only be happy when I wear a habit.

"I love you both." I kiss them on the head. "Call us if anything happens."

They call goodbyes after me. I walk outside, where I know Dante will be picking me up in two minutes. He sleeps in my bed, but he still insists on picking me up for proper dates. He says a gentleman has to.

A sleek, black sports car pulls up, and Dante grins.

"Mid-life already?" I ask, pulling a scarf out of my purse to tie my hair.

"Work went well," he replies.

He already takes the twists and curves of Greek cliffs like a native. By the end of the ride, I'm certain I've cried my mascara off, and my cheeks hurt from the wind pulling them back. But he's laughing like a kid, like he never laughed in New York, so I can't complain.

At the door, he greets a man in a short-sleeved button-down and slacks. "Iason! I brought the wife, as promised."

Iason glances at me, then does an exaggerated double-take. "Apologies, friend, I can't seat you. I'd risk the wrath of Aphrodite, allowing such a beautiful woman inside."

The two of them laugh like it's an inside joke, and I realize suddenly that Dante's shirt is gray, and his tie is the same blue as my dress. His suit is even charcoal. How long has it been since I saw him in all black?

I don't miss it.

Despite his complaints, Iason seats us at apparently the best table in his restaurant, outside overlooking the cliffs. Dante and I hold hands throughout the meal.

He raises his glass. "To your last semester, and to being the first Calimeris to graduate college."

I knock my wine against his with a smile. "I'll feel better in a week. How's Tasia taking my absence?"

"Hard, as always." He sips his wine and nods. "But Mama knows to hire some extra help around this time now."

Everything is routine here. Sometimes, our life in New York City feels like a dream. I rub my thumb across the scar in the center of Dante's palm.

"Still happy at the restaurant?"

Dante feigns hurt. "Come on, El, I'd tell you. And with our little monster running around, it's not like I'm ever going to get bored."

Years ago, when we'd just moved to Greece, I was getting settled at NTU, Gregorio's was threatening to go bust, and Dante's injuries from his Russian captivity were slowing him down. I'd told him point-blank that we were a one-kid family. Tasia, as a newborn, was too much trouble. I wondered if we'd made the wrong decision by leaving the life, moving away from the city we'd grown up in, and leaving good friends who became family behind.

But as I look out over the cliffs, a feeling of rightness fills me.

"You know how I said we were a one-kid family?" I ask.

He raises an eyebrow.

"What if we weren't?" I stare into his eyes, looking for any flicker of worry or disappointment.

Bold, brash excitement shines back at me, covered in a thick helping of love. "If I say I was waiting for you to ask, does that make me sound like a pig?"

"Depends." I grin. "Are you excited about having a baby, or making a baby?"

Dante slides a hand up my leg, dislodging the silky fabric. "Both."

"I love you." I kiss him softly, that warmth buoying all my movements. "So much."

"I love you too." Dante raises his free hand. "Can we get the check?"

My laughter rings out over the Grecian waves.

5 0

TONY'S STORY

TONY

"You're supposed to stop the Q-Tip when you feel resistance, jackass," I say into the phone. "When I say Tuesday, I mean fucking Tuesday, not next Thursday."

"Sorry, Mr. Bellini," the importer on the other end of the line mutters. "I guess I heard you wrong. But I can't—"

"Can't," I repeat. "Last guy who used the word 'can't' with me didn't live long enough to regret it. So, my cars? On Tuesday?"

"Tuesday, Mr. Bellini," he says.

I hang up and stretch. We gotta get a new space. I've been working on this basement underneath Lou's Deli for the past two fucking years, and it still looks like a deli basement. Sure, the meat hooks give it a certain menacing energy, but the smell of cold cuts takes that right out. And I can hear Lou's kid's punk music through the part directly under their house sometimes, no matter how much sound-proofing I put up. I shut my laptop.

It's seven, so I should be getting home. Federica—Freddie, she says—will be waiting for me to start dinner. Honest to God, I don't know how Dante survived so long with how little staff he had. I can't imagine going home to a house as big as either of ours and knowing it's going to be empty.

My phone vibrates. I check the message.

Meet me in the city for a drink tonight or I'll sic as many Kings as I can find in five minutes on yer ass. Thought I was getting a chattier don in you.

Cal Duncan, who is pronouncedly as much of an ass as he was the moment I met him, though a lot less dangerous. The worst thing his boys would do to me is piss me off. Still, as much as I know Freddie's waiting, whatever tacky bar he chooses might actually be better than going home and looking at syndicate shit all night. Maybe I'll pick someone up. I have been bored.

Fine, I reply with a smirk.

He's been bothering me about this for weeks. He should know a comment about chattiness is going to get something like that in return. I slide my phone into my pocket and head up the stairs into the deli proper. The smell of cold cuts does not get better.

Two years have passed, but sometimes it feels like two weeks. Like the Saints are still in a goddamn holding pattern. I'm leading us well. We got all the territory we agreed upon in the Russian play, and I've wheedled a little more out of Cal here and there. But we're not growing. We still don't even have a goddamn club.

Time to pull my head out of my ass and stop wasting time. I wave briefly to Lou and escape into an alley—garbage stink, even more pleasant—then out onto the street proper. My car sits there. My nice, clean car, where I will be trapped with all the smells that stain my days now.

Pass. I'll take the ferry, maybe make Cal pick me up. The city hasn't been at war in ages.

On the walk to the shore, I place calls and send emails. A few of them are running Saints business. The rest are new. A realtor Dante left me, to look for more club properties. Carla, who used to run Piacere, for her expertise. Anyone else I can think of who might have a bright new idea.

The ghost of Seb threatens. I don't see him like I did in the days right after his death, but he's never far from my mind. Tonight, he's laughing at me for taking this goddamn long. I shrug him off and catch the ferry just before it pulls away from the dock.

Lower floor is packed, so I head to the upper. I'm here for the breeze, anyway. A gaggle of women in tiny dresses shriek with laughter. Oh, great. A group of—I glance at their hair—Staten Island locals, determined to make jackasses of themselves in the big city. Honestly, I'm just surprised one of them doesn't have a "bride-to-be" or "twenty-one" sash on, with the way they're behaving. I roll my eyes and twist to edge past them, up to the railing where I really want to be.

Perfect timing. One of them drops a little black purse right in my path. I step on it, hear something crack, and wince. They might be tacky and irritating, but I'm not a monster. I bend down to grab the bag and offer to pay for whatever I broke.

At the same moment, what I assume to be the owner of the bag also bends down. I smash my forehead into her chin.

"Fuck." I wince and try to get out of the way so she can stand. "Sorry, uh—"

The woman straightens, and I recognize her immediately, even though it's been, shit, like a year and a half since I've seen her. Chloe. Same pale blonde hair, same cornflower blue eyes, same kissable little dent in her lower lip.

"Tony," she says.

Breathlessly?

No. I'm imagining shit now. It's probably because I damn near smashed her teeth in.

"Been a while," I say.

She nods. "You've been too busy for most of the Saints activities lately."

"Yeah." I rub my aching forehead. "Uh, I can pay for your—" I look at the crushed remains of the bag. It seems what cracked was some kind of skeleton holding the whole thing together. "Purse."

She glances over her shoulder, then opens it to show a cracked phone and splattered lip gloss inside.

"And the rest of it," I say quickly. Fuck, aren't I supposed to be the smooth one? There's just something about her that makes me feel like my lines would bounce right off.

She steps away from her group. "You know, I really shouldn't go into the city without a phone."

"Makes sense." I grimace. "You want mine?"

"That depends." She looks up at me with those blue, blue eyes. "What are your plans tonight?"

Deciding to forget Cal Duncan is easy. It may well be my natural state of being. "You know, suddenly they just opened up."

Chloe smiles.

End of Book 3

Thank you for reading! Book four is in the works and will be out soon! Keep reading for Chapter 1

BOOK 4 CHAPTER 1: BAD NEWS

Tony

The cold glass touches my lips as I sip from my whiskey, my eyes watching Estella over the rim. She's dancing in front of a group of fucking loud guys who came here for a bachelor party. I'm in my usual booth at Aphrodite's Lounge, and even though she's a hell of a dancer, I can't seem to keep my focus on her for more than a few seconds tonight.

This is a clear sign that I'm losing interest in her, no matter how hot and good at sex she is. In all honesty, I'm getting bored of her.

And it's not like I should feel guilty about it since I know she only likes my money anyway—like all of them do. But as much as I like to have women keeping me company every once in a while–especially when I need to blow off some steam–Estella is not managing to entertain me any longer.

I rub my temples, trying to make this fucking headache that's been gwaning on me for the past three days go away. Estella's gaze finds mine from across the club, and I fight the urge to look away. I have no intention of indulging her tonight, but I don't want to be rude either.

A couple of patrons walk past my booth and wave at me, their drinks in hand as they head to the VIP section at the far end of the room. I greet them by raising my glass, recognizing them from a few other nights, but not bothering to give them an ounce of a smile.

Estella's dance is coming to an end. I can tell that by the way those fucking losers are waving their dollar bills at her, one of them attempting to slide one under her thong shorts hem. She smiles seductively at them, noticing the amount of money she'll be taking home.

If I want to escape her tonight, I need to get out of here before the song ends. I won't be able to tell her no if she approaches this booth and sits on my lap, no matter how bored I am of her.

I turn the remnants of my glass down my throat, feeling the liquid burning my windpipe, and stand up, heading toward the back door without looking back. I pop open the button on my suit jacket, feeling it too tight and uncomfortable all of a sudden.

My black SUV is in the club's private parking lot, and thankfully I don't bump into anyone on my way out. I ponder heading home, but there's still work to be done tonight that can't be postponed anymore. For the past four years, it has felt like my days are endless and filled with countless shit to handle. It's a fucking rollercoaster with no end in sight.

Whenever I come close to having a glimpse of peace, something happens to start it all over again.

Another problem to be solved; another business deal to close...

It never ends.

So, with that in mind, I go back to Lou's Deli instead.

No, I haven't gotten out of that hole yet. In fact, as much as I hated it when I took over from Dante as the new head of the Saints, the space kind of grew on me with time. I don't even gag at the smell of cold cuts anymore. I don't even feel it, to be fair, my nose already used to it by now.

It is spacious after all, and after looking over the entire city for a better place, nothing seemed to convince me to move our headquarters from there, so we simply stayed. It's been serving us right so far.

The street is dark and empty as I step out of the car and walk inside. It is too damn late, so I shouldn't be expecting the place to be on full function. It feels odd to find this place completely empty, with not a single soul around.

As soon as I get to the deli's basement, I notice there is no one here either.

It is better this way anyway. I work better on my own; just utter silence keeping me company–and the voices in my head, reminding me of darker times and nightmares from the past. Seb's voice is one of them, still visiting me when I least expect it. My visions of him are not as frequent as they used to be, but I still see him.

I walk over to my office and round my wooden desk, finding it covered with stacks of paperwork. I shuffle through them, searching for what I need to work on tonight. The inventory being shipped out tomorrow has to be checked and approved by me before heading off the port, so I need to handle this before going home.

It's lost on me why I procrastinated so far to do that, but it's no one else's fault but my own. This file has been on my desk for at least a week now, so I can't put the blame on anyone else today.

When I finally find the document I need, I plop down in my chair, urging my brain to function properly so I make no mistakes. I fucking hate the detailed and thorough part of this job. But as much as I'd love to have one of the guys do it for me, there are things that require my eyes only. No one else's.

So, I lose myself on the endless list of numbers and names, papers in one hand and a pen in the other.

Footsteps echoing on porcelain tiles a few minutes later–or has it been hours?–make me snap my head up and crease my brows in confusion. I glance at my watch, which reads 3:00 AM.

Who the fuck is here at this hour?

"I figured I'd find you here." Armando's voice reaches me before I can even see him. My second steps into the doorway, his face hooded by shadows since I only have one lamp lit on my desk. I can tell he's tired by the way his dark circles are evident even from this distance, but he's looking sleek as always in his black suit.

"Aren't you supposed to be at home with your wife and kids?" I ask with a frown, leaning back in my chair, watching as he walks inside the room. His footsteps are heavy and loud, especially since I've been hearing nothing but the ticking of the clock and the shuffle of paper for the past two hours.

"I'm afraid I have some bad news that couldn't wait until tomorrow, Boss," he tells me, sitting on the chair across from me.

"Couldn't you have called?"

Armando shakes his head, his jaw clenched slightly. "It's delicate news, so I thought you'd prefer that I delivered it personally."

He's right. Armando is extremely attentive to how I like things to be done, not to mention overly cautious, which is a good quality to have in this type of business.

"All right, just fucking tell me then. What happened?" I press, getting impatient with all his rambling and unnecessary suspense.

"I just got a call from Nicky Bertolucci," he starts gloomily. "Apparently, Carlo had a heart attack this afternoon and died at his house in Miami."

I stare blankly at him, taking in the news. Not that I cared too much about Carlo because I damn well know he didn't like me. When I took over the Saints, he didn't agree with me being the new boss. So, faster than lightning, he retired and moved to Miami with his wife and daughter.

He had worked with Dante's father for longer than I've been alive. He had good networking and good insight on how things were done, so it was a great loss to our businesses.

But if he didn't trust me, he was better off elsewhere. I couldn't risk having someone with me who might stab me in the back at any moment.

But I do feel sorry for his wife and daughter.

Nicky and Chloe Bertolucci.

Pale blonde, cornflower blue eyes Chloe.

Chloe, who I haven't seen since we met at a ferry going into the city and drunkenly ended up having sex with–Chloe.

"The Bertolucci family has a plot in the local cemetery and the mob wives are getting together in the morning to start planning the funeral," Armando continues, pulling me back from my trip down memory lane. "Nicky is having his body shipped back for the burial. I wasn't sure if you knew about it or not yet. That's why I came here to tell you."

Again, he did the right thing. It never hurts to be too careful.

It's not like our lives are a fucking fairy tale.

One missed step and we're as good as dead.

I rub my neck, trying to think of what to do.

"Tell them I'll pay for the funeral," I tell him bluntly, not wanting to go further into details. I don't want to know about any of it now. I don't want to know about how Chloe is. It's been two fucking years since I heard from her, and it is better this way. "In fact, I'll charter a private jet for the Bertolucci women and Carlo."

I still find myself daydreaming about her, against my will, and I don't know if it's a good thing or not that I can barely remember the night we spent together. I still find myself wanting to remember the details of her lying naked in my bed, the soft feel of her skin under mine, the way her smooth blonde hair felt on my fingers, the way she moaned my name over and over until she was out of breath and wasted beneath me.

I haven't been able to stop thinking about her since, wondering how she is and if she ever thinks about me the same way. I feel like a fucking teenager fantasizing about having her again and again. Night after night.

No matter how many dancers I get in my bed, none of them makes me forget her. Her sweet, floral scent. That is one thing that I could never forget.

It hurt my ego to not have her reach out to me and come looking for me after that night, but I can't blame her for not wanting to have anything to do with this life anymore.

Moving away from this city—and from me—was the best thing she could have done.

Armando is looking at me with an enigmatic face, but he knows better than to ask me about whatever it is he's thinking.

"See that they have everything they need." I carry on, ignoring the way my stomach twists when I imagine Chloe's blue eyes filled with tears as she mourns her father. "And let me know when it's happening so I can be there to offer my condolences."

"You're going to be there?" Armando asks, his tone serious but wary. "Do you think that's wise? Who knows who might show up, Boss?"

It's not like I can miss the funeral of a former member of the Saints. Especially as their new boss.

I nod. "Carlo used to work for the Saints. I need to pay my respects. It's the right thing to do."

I don't tell him that I'm also secretly eager to see Chloe again, even if I have to watch her crying from afar, not able to do anything to comfort her.

Banter of the Devil (releases 10/15/2024)

The Mafia Kings series

Indebted to the Mafia King

<u>Loved by the Mafia King</u> (releases 9/15/2024)

Claimed by the Mafia King (releases 11/15/2024)

Sign up for Bella's newsletter here.

Follow Bella on Facebook here.

www.ingramcontent.com/pod-product-compliance
Lightning Source LLC
Chambersburg PA
CBHW070415310726
48977CB00003B/702